SQUAD GIGANTIC

GO GET EM!

J. Andrade

Published by Gigantic Chronicles Ltd
www.SquadGigantic.com

ISBN: 978-1-9999457-0-1

Printed For Gigantic Chronicles Ltd

Contents

"A drop of rain is nothing on its own, but when they form together it's a storm… Work together as one"

- Big J

Chapter 1 - Paradise Mountains

⫫Welcome Mr Gigantic" Said Chief Danjuma, The leader of All Tribes.

"Please call me Jay, it's an honour to be given the privilege of entering the... how do you say it? Ip-har-adisi Inzin-ta-ba" replied Jay trying to pronounce the name of this euphoric environment whilst he looked around in amazement.

Chief Danjuma smiled and said

"You've done your homework I see, but honestly just call it Paradise Mountains, I appreciate you using the native name of our home... but feel free to also use your tongue Ipharadisi Inzintaba or Paradise Mountains will do fine"

Chief Danjuma led the way followed by two of his Mountain Guards and Jay. They began a tour of Paradise Mountains. As they walked, Chief Danjuma explained the structure and rituals behind this sacred place. "Although Paradise Mountains is virtually impossible to be found by man, it's actually the centre of the Earth" said the Chief with a stern yet welcoming tone "This is where every aspect of nature comes from".

"Everything?" asked Jay.

"Yes, everything. From animals to vegetables, from humans to minerals, gases to even mathematical and scientific equations. EVERYTHING!" said Chief Danjuma.

Looking excited and amazed, Jay began to ask

questions which he believed he already had the answers to, but he still asked because he couldn't let the opportunity to confirm these folk tales pass him.

"My mother told me stories about Paradise Mountains all my life. I hear its waters are so pure it can heal all diseases known to man with just two sips?" "Yes, that's true" replied the Chief.

"I've also been told that the city is owned by three tribes; The Tribe of Strength, The Tribe of Creativity and the Tribe of Nature" continued Jay.

"This is also true" said Chief Danjuma with a smirk, amused by the joy in Jay's face and the childlike attitude he showed whilst questioning him.

"I've also heard that there are special gemstones created by The Paradise Mountains which possess special powers; powers that have the ability to rule the World!"

The Chief interrupted and said "Whoa, whoa, whoa... slow down" whilst looking over to his guards with a facial expression which showed discomfort. "Many things you have been informed of are true, but unfortunately this one is just a fairy tale; a simple myth" responded the Chief.

With a face of disappointment Jay said, "So is the story of the four children destined to save the World and bring justice, equality and peace to all just a myth too?" "I'm afraid so Mr Gigantic" said the Chief as he continued the tour.

Jay was disappointed for a second or two, he was upset to hear that he had been fed lies all his life. Jay had learned about Paradise Mountains since he was a child. Each night his mother would rock him to sleep telling him stories of this beautiful place and he continued to be told these stories up to this day. Jay dreamed of being invited to the Paradise Mountains; the most sacred place on Earth. The place where everything on Earth originates from: civilisation, technology, agriculture, science... everything and anything you could imagine.

Not any and everybody is able to enter the Paradise Mountains, the Mountains are spiritually protected. The only two ways you can be granted access is if you are a direct descendent of the tribes or by direct invite from the Chief himself; an invite which is only extended based on your integrity, honour and righteousness! This was the reason why Jay Gigantic was so overwhelmed and honoured to be here.

Jay Gigantic was a business man from London who lived a hard life. As a teenager he was constantly caught up in bad situations but always acted with a good clean heart. Jay was a hustler who just tried to survive day by day. He taught himself Mixed Martial Arts to defend himself from gangs and gangsters on the gritty streets of London.

Growing up on the streets of South London wasn't easy, but Jay always took comfort in believing if he could make it there, he could make it anywhere. As Jay got older he noticed the error of his ways and made the necessary changes. He vowed to become a business man, not just any business man but the most successful business man in the World with the aim of bettering the lives of anyone he comes in to contact with. Armed with nothing but a pound and a dream, Jay decided to build his empire and since that day he never looked back.

"Come this way Mr Gigantic" said Chief Danjuma.

The Chief put his arm on Jay's shoulder and led him to a deep colourful waterfall. The waterfall looked unreal. It was an array of colours with each strand of water looking like thousands of diamonds falling gently into a sea of rainbows.

Worrying he would be drenched by the waterfall, Jay quickly stopped in his tracks and with a gleeful but confused look he said, "This way yeah... you sure?"

The Chief's Guards laughed and one finally broke his silence to say "The English boy is scared".

"SILENCE!!!" said the Chief, striking instant fear into his guards. "A brave man is merely a fool who acts without reasoning, a courageous man is a man of wisdom who questions his actions then goes ahead with the choice he has made" preached the Chief.

Jay smiled, feeling confident that he had the Chief on his side. Jay then looked at the guards and said, "Yeah, you hear that? This English boy's courageous. You better respect my name! Hahahaha". "Let's not speak too fast. You are yet to make your decision Mr Gigantic" said the Chief, humbling Jay.

With the smile wiped off of his face, Jay looked at the majestic waterfall and thought, Why not?!

Something about Paradise Mountains made Jay feel at home. Jay strongly believed in following his instincts and his instincts told him he can be at ease and demonstrate trust.

Jay was experiencing a feeling he couldn't explain, it was like he was amongst family. He took a long hard look at the waterfall and thought to himself, "This water can only be a good thing, it heals everything in a couple of sips. Imagine what a full body wash can do". Jay giggled to himself then looked Chief Danjuma dead in his eyes and said, "Let's do it!"

"Wise Choice" said the Chief as he took a giant leap into the waterfall.

In an effort to keep up, Jay closed his eyes and also took a giant leap of faith into the waterfall.

Jay was still pretty nervous, but of all the things that should've been running through his mind, the only thing he thought was 'I only brought these creps' a few days ago, this waters gonna' ruin them!'

"Arrgggghhh!" shouted Jay as he jumped in, then he opened his eyes and to his surprise he wasn't wet at all and there was no great fall either.

"Well done Mr Gigantic. In life the hardest thing is to take the courageous first step, one day you'll realise that step you just took was the biggest step in your life... Now your real visit can begin!" said the Chief.

Jay just laughed, half in relief and the other half shocked that the Chief tricked him.

The Chief is a serious faced man, a wise older guy; a wise older guy you know not to mess with! Jay could see that everyone around the Chief saw the Chief as the leader, like a father figure to the whole of Paradise Mountains.

Chief Danjuma's face showed he was a man of age, but his body and ability to manoeuvre was as fit, solid and healthy as a twenty five year old gladiator.

Everything about Chief Danjuma demanded your respect.

"Here is the true Paradise Mountains, this is the home of the three tribes. This is where the stories you have been told since birth stem from" said Chief Danjuma.

Jay was stunned and amazed by what was in front of him. The beauty in the area before the waterfall was enough for Jay to love Paradise Mountains, so to think that was technically Paradise Mountains lobby entrance totally blew his mind.

Jay couldn't help thinking what had he done to deserve to be invited into Paradise Mountains. He thought 'out of billions of people in the World, why me?'

Jay couldn't contain his thought any longer and before taking another step he came to a halt and said "Why me, why have I been chosen to witness this?"

"In life be patient and all will be revealed" said the Chief.

Jay didn't really know how to take that response, but the Chief wasn't the type of guy that you questioned. Jay walked around in awe, astonished by how advanced Paradise Mountains were. He was constantly asking the Chief's Guards questions about everything he saw. The technology was lightyears ahead of anything Jay had seen in London or anywhere else in the World.

The Chief said "Anything good that's to be introduced to the World is invented and tested here first, then it's given to the World once we are completely satisfied it'll benefit the planet".

Jay spent days travelling around Paradise Mountains seeing all the fascinating sites and attributes it possessed. Jay met members from each of the tribes and strangely they all greeted him as if they knew him already and strangely he felt the same way about them too. Jay ate with the tribes and played with the children enjoying the unity of Paradise Mountains. He met with Chief Danjuma's wife - Jenay, she was a beautiful woman. She had him mesmerised by her beauty and subtle strength. Jenay was also extremely healthy for her age, in fact the only physical attribute that gave away her age was the perfectly placed grey strands of hair that streaked through her dreadlocks, shining like platinum adding to the simplicity of her beauty.

Jay found Jenay to have an intriguing resemblance to his mother. This automatically made him take to her spirit and soul.

Jenay made Jay feel extremely welcomed, she asked him personal questions like

"Do you have a wife? Have you got any children?"

Jay respectfully replied "No not yet".

"Why not? A handsome man like you! You should at least be seeing a lovely lady," said Jenay whilst giving Jay a sharp look of concern. "You should be in wedlock with little Jays running around, I don't understand you young boys and girls nowadays" rambled on Jenay whilst seasoning the chicken for dinner.

Jay smiled and laughed to himself, he never had any grandparents growing up and imagined that this must be exactly what it feels like having a discussion with your granny.

"I hear you're pretty handy in the kitchen Jay" said Jenay whilst inviting him into the kitchen area.

"Yeah you heard correct" said Jay with a smug grin.

"Well get in here boy" said Jenay with a proud smile.

Jay and Jenay spent the afternoon cooking and talking about anything that came to mind. Jenay spoke words of wisdom with a firm but caring delivery. Jay's heart instantly grew fond of Jenay and a special bond was immediately formed.

After eating the meal they cooked together, Jenay and Chief Danjuma took Jay up to the mountains to a place they called 'The Eye of Paradise'. The Eye of Paradise was exactly what its name suggested; this was the most central and highest point of the city within the mountains. When Chief Danjuma, Jenay and Jay arrived at the Eye of Paradise they were greeted by the Watcher who was on duty. Chief Danjuma explained there is a team of seven highly spiritual guards who take shifts watching over the city and foreseeing any threats to the Paradise Mountains.

The Watcher went to a side with Chief Danjuma and whispered something into his ear with a worried looked on his face. The Chief replied, "I've sensed it for a while and we will be ready". The Chief then re-joined Jay and Jenay.

The views were astonishing, there were rainbows made of coloured gemstones shooting out of the ground and bouncing over the city reflecting into the waters. There were Star Diamonds and Red Painites in abundance alongside some of the World's other most rare gemstones which were just growing like weeds in a garden. Jay couldn't believe his eyes. It was like a wonderland, he slyly pinched himself to see if he was dreaming.

Jenay went into a little box she had and took out an elegant cloth that was made from the softest fabric Jay had ever set his eyes upon. The cloth had a special sophisticated design that was crazily familiar to Jay. Jenay opened the cloth and inside was a Fire Red Diamond, it was the most enchanting and exquisite diamond he had ever seen. A red tone shun through the diamond with what looked like a gentle flame glowing in the centre.

"WOW!" said Jay with that same childish look on his face. Then he went on to say, "That's one of the rarest gems in the World you know. I didn't even think it really existed. That's worth a bag of cash!"

"It is, but its value is worth much more than any amount of money in the World" replied Jenay as she slowly placed the Fire Red Diamond in Jay's hand.
Chief Danjuma interrupted and said "This Fire Red Diamond is the only one in the World and it's yours Jay".
"Promise us that you will never sell the Fire Red Diamond no matter the offer you may receive and also promise you will guard it with your life. It is extremely important, more important than you can currently imagine!" said Jenay whilst giving Jay the same serious and sincere look that the Chief gives him.
Jay was overwhelmed with honour. He replied "I'll protect it with everything I've got, I promise!" Jenay

and Chief Danjuma then went on to point out the homes of the Tribes in Paradise Mountains explaining the roles and importance of each one.

"Straight ahead of you is The Tribe of Nature. This Tribe's main attributes are the intelligence of man and the understanding of nature. Everything that keeps humanity alive and moving is here. Technology, fuels, food, education, maths, science, literature, that thing you call the internet... everything, it's the most important of the tribes" said Jenay.

"To the left is The Tribe of Strength, the power behind all things. They are the chosen protectors of the World, the enforcers of justice and the natural labourers." "So what's that smaller area to the right? They look lit!" said Jay whilst pointing to what looked like a party town.

"Since I've been here they've been doing bits, they look like they're having nothing but fun" laughed Jay. "That's the Tribe of Creativity. I guess to the naked eye it looks like the most fun of the tribes and they are as you say... Lit'" said the Chief trying to make sense of Jay's slang.

"However, it all depends on how the individual looks at things" said the Chief making Jay think deeply about his comment.

Chief Danjuma then went on to say "This tribe brings entertainment and joy, making the World a happy and fun place to live in. Happiness and joy is the best medicine in life, all the World's top entertainers, athletes and anything of that sort are descendants of this tribe".

As Jay soaked in the environment and all that was told to him, he looked behind and noticed another area which was as big as all the tribes towns put together "What area is that then?" Asked Jay. Sternly looking into

Jay's eyes, the Chief stated "That's what we call the Forbidden Area, the average citizen of Paradise Mountains is forbidden to enter as it possesses a energy so pure and strong that its dangerous! This area also holds ancient secrets that is not to be tampered with". The seriousness in the Chief's face and tone made Jay know he wasn't to ask any more questions on the subject.

Jay had a great day; it was like all the stories he had been told as a child had come to life. However, he still couldn't get his head around the Fire Red Diamond.

Jay battled with his mind thinking 'Why did they give it to me? Does it possess any powers? Am I really going to be able to protect this? Do I even deserve it???'

He had so many thoughts and questions which were sending his brain off in all different directions. Jay's final thought was 'No matter what the reason is, I will rise to the challenge and honour the wishes of Chief Danjuma and Jenay'.

Chapter 2 - Trouble In Paradise

It was Jay's last day in the Paradise Mountains. The Chief came and met him at the guest quarters, then they went for a stroll after eating a feast of a breakfast.

Something felt a little different but Jay couldn't put his finger on it, he couldn't figure out exactly what it was, but he could definitely feel something in the air. Instead of questioning the vibe he was feeling, Jay just bypassed it and put it down to him being upset that he was leaving this perfect place.

"Jay" said Chief Danjuma.

Now things were really strange, 'The Chief hasn't called me by my first name once whilst I've been here' thought Jay.

Jay felt he had finally gained the Chief's trust.

"I hope you've enjoyed your stay" said Chief Danjuma.

"Every moment of it Chief, I wish I could've stayed longer" replied Jay.

"Well remember you are welcome here anytime" said the Chief as he stared deeply in to Jay's eyes then said "Look at this as your home".

Jay saw the sincerity in the Chief's eyes, he felt honoured and privileged to be told this. Chief Danjuma then went on to say, "There are still many more things that you must learn about the Paradise Mountains".

"I can imagine" said Jay.

"Seriously much more, not only about Paradise Mountains... but also about you too!" said the Chief.

Jay was baffled, he squinted his eyes and said, "What d'you mean?"

The Chief stopped and turned to Jay saying, "You are...".

Then just as the Chief was about to complete his sentence, at least ten of his army came running and shouting "CHIEF DANJUMA!"

A few of the guards were bloody, some with their own blood and some with the blood of others dripping of their knuckles and armour.

"Chief I'm afraid the day has come!" said the Chief's most trusted guard Santago.

Jay stood there glassy eyed and a bit taken aback.

'What could've happened?' thought Jay, 'This place is Paradise!'

"I know" said Chief Danjuma. He then said, "I've sensed it for a while now and prophecy always has a funny way of fulfilling itself".

"I don't know what's going on, but whatever it is I'm ridin'!" Said an anxious and scared Jay, the previous confusion had passed and a natural instinct to protect what he loves kicked in.

"Now is not a time to be brave Jay, it's a time to be courageous and wise..." said the Chief.

"Huh?" replied Jay.

"Courage and wisdom outlives bravery a hundred times over. Prophecy has a major task ahead for you" said Chief Danjuma.

"Bang's attack is gaining strength Chief, we really must act now!" shouted Santago.

"BANG?! Marlo Bang?" Asked Jay.

"Yes" said the Chief again looking deep into Jay's eyes, but this time as an attempt to keep Jay calm.

"Santago, ring the alarm and strike back with our full army… even those who are not fully trained! Ensure the Gemstones and the Chosen Children are safely escorted to Jay's plane" commanded the Chief.

"Yes Chief" said the loyal Santago.

"…and Santago, no matter what happens The Chosen Children, the gemstones and Jay are of the most importance! No one and nothing else matters as much as them! Not me, not ANYONE! Do you understand?"

"Yes Chief, I understand" said Santago with a slight look of fear.

"Jay come with me, I need to lock the Waterfall" commanded the Chief.

Jay ran with the Chief until the majestical Waterfall that Jay entered the Paradise Mountains through was in sight. The Chief stopped, closed his eyes and then aimed the palms of his hands at the Waterfall, it was at this moment Jay witnessed one of the most breathtaking sights ever! As the Chief pointed his hands he conjured up a massive glow which eventually shot over to the Waterfall and piece by piece pulled all the flowing water that resembled colourful diamonds together, the diamond like liquid formed into one massive diamond like barrier which sealed the entrance to the Paradise Mountains.

"That should hold them off for a while" said the Chief as he ran back towards the main city to command his army.

"What the hell is going on? What's Bang doing here?" shouted Jay as they ran along side a few of the Chief's Guards.

The Chief then said "Do you remember what you said about the four children destined to save the World?"

"Yeah" said an intrigued Jay.

"...And the gemstones?" said the Chief

"Yeah" said Jay whilst slowly nodding his head.

"THEY ARE ALL TRUE! The part you didn't know is that the children and gemstones will need to be protected by another Chosen One at least until they are adults".

As Jay tried to process his thoughts of amazement, Chief Danjuma said "...and that particular Chosen One is YOU!"

Jay stopped and said "WHAT?"

The Chief then went on to explain to Jay, "Jay this is not a time to stop, we are in the middle of a war. Your childhood friend Marlo Bang has been on a quest for worldwide domination! Bang's been gathering precious gemstones from mountains all over the World. The only gemstones he doesn't have are the ones connected to the Chosen Children and you!"

"What happens if he gets them all?" Asked Jay.

"That's simple, they will connect and he will take over the World, ruling it with greed and destruction!" said the Chief with a look of sorrow.

Jay looked around and said "Well we can't let that happen... give me a gun big man".

Chief Danjuma's guards looked at Jay in shock.

"What? Why are you lot looking at me like that?" said a confused Jay.

"In war they shoot at you and you shoot back until someone wins" stated Jay.

"We don't use guns, guns are created by those of destruction, not of us" said Chief Danjuma.

"Well right now I need something!" said Jay in frustration.

"We don't believe in guns" said a guard.

"Well let me tell you this, they are very real! And Bang's about to get rid of us... probably using his big selection of them!" replied Jay.

The Chief just laughed as things got worse.

SMASHHHHHH!!! One of Bang's men had fists made of rock and completely smashed through the locked Waterfall with just a few mighty big boulder rocks he shot out his hands!

"Good on ya' Thug Rock" said Bang. "Dealer take a few

men and search for those Gems!" commanded Bang as they ran through and launched their attack.

The Waterfall had now completely given way and shattered into a stream of crushed diamonds. Jay's heart fell as he watched the beautiful waterfall crumble.

"Do not fear Jay, we have a few tricks up our sleeves too" said the Chief in a confident tone.

"Well feel free to show me some anytime soon" replied Jay whilst jumping over the carnage attempting to get to his plane.

"We protect ourselves with our gifted powers and strength that has derived from nature" said Chief Danjuma. Then he spun round and took out three of Bang's men with one swift flying kick manoeuvre.

It was as if the Chief glided through the air. This was the first time Jay witnessed some of the powers and abilities from the Paradise Mountains.

Jay was astonished, but there was no time to admire the Chief and his guards fighting skills as Jay now found himself in battle too!

One of Bang's soldiers grabbed Jay from behind and put him in a raw naked choke whilst another punched him in the stomach. Jay sucked up the punches and managed to stand straight, he then lifted his leg and axe kicked the soldier in front of him. Jay flipped the other soldier over his back then ground and pounded him. Jay's years of Mixed Martial Arts training proved to be a blessing. He went on to take out at least four of Bang's fighters using a combination of elbow strikes, hammer fist and a swift exhibition of dirty boxing.

Bang's squad came with an arsenal of guns and automatic weapons but their weapons were pointless as they couldn't work in Paradise Mountains sacred lands. However, Bang was prepared! He loaded his army with machetes and vicious animals such as battle trained Lions, Wolves and Panthers!

Jay knew Bang well as they grew up together as best friends in the hood.

As children Bang and Jay were next door neighbours and attended the same primary school. In the past, they would have each other's backs on the roads through thick and thin even though they would always clash due to Bang's greed and selfish ways.

As they grew older their relationship came to an abrupt end as Bang betrayed Jay in a dodgy business deal which could have potentially put Jay's life at risk. Instead of taking responsibility for his wrongs, Bang disappeared from the area and swore Jay was now his enemy for life!

Chapter 3 - Raheem, Rhiarn, Danny and Jerome

In a distance Jay could see Santago and a few of the Chief's Guards in combat with Bang and his army of fighters. Bang's numbers were strong but so was Santago and the guards! They were going through Bang's team two by two and three by three, but Bang's men refused to be defeated and they just kept coming!

Finally Santago and his men got through the flurry of Bang's soldiers. Jay looked over and saw Santago had four children standing behind him; the oldest child couldn't have been older than twelve years old and the smallest child looked as young as eight years old.

Amazingly these children showed no signs of fear as they stood in the middle of the battlefield.

When Jay initially saw the children, he thought 'Why are they here? They shouldn't be seeing this'.

Then it all made sense… 'They must be the Chosen Children.'

Straight away Jay felt a natural urge to get to the children and protect them from the mayhem. He ran straight over to them, disposing of any one of Bang's men that got in his way.

As Jay approached Santago and the children, Chief

Danjuma said "I don't know how much longer we can hold off Bang's soldiers... their attack is too strong!" "Jay, I have something to give you" said the Chief. Jay thought 'What could it be?' Surely the Fire Red Diamond was enough.

Chief Danjuma said "Take this bag" whilst handing Jay a bag made out of the same extremely soft material that the Fire Red Diamond was presented in."Inside are four precious gemstones, each gem is connected to each one of the Chosen Children" said the Chief.

Jay took the bag and tried his best to listen closely to every word the Chief said, but he kept getting distracted by the war.

"Ignore your surroundings and focus Jay!" said the Chief in a stern voice whilst gripping him firmly to get his attention.

"Not only are the gemstones connected to the children, they are also connected to you and your Fire Red Diamond. If the gems happen to separate from each other the flame in your fire will extinguish bit by bit and relight in the soul of an evil being. That evil being will then become unstoppable with ultimate power that they will use to rule the World! YOU CAN NOT ALLOW THIS TO HAPPEN!" Said Chief Danjuma as clear as he could possibly be.

"I understand" said a now attentive Jay.

Out of nowhere a machete as long as an arm came flying towards Jay. The Chief pushed Jay out of harms way at the cost of the machete ripping into his own shoulder.

Fearing the worst outcome of the battle, Jay looked at the Chief and said "Chief are you OK? What shall I do?"

"GET THE CHILDREN TO THE PLANE!" Shouted Chief Danjuma as he pulled the blade out his arm and launched it through the air, right back at Bang's men whilst charging back into battle with them.

Jay took the youngest child by his hand to lead him away.

"Wow, that's a strong grip lil' man" said Jay confused as to how this little boy could have such a firm hold.

Then a deep voice, one of a grown man projected from the eight year olds vocal chords.

"I'm from the Tribe of Strength… it's kinda' what we do" replied the boy as he laughed.

Then he went on to say, "Trust me, you don't need to hold my hand" as he released his grip.

This little boy was Jerome, but his height was the only thing little about him! Apart from his cute chubby cheeks, his body was already as solid as rock with muscles that would make the World's best body builder jealous.

A few of the Chief's guards came back and took over his fight as he walked back to Jay and the children.

"Children go with him" said Chief Danjuma.

"This is Jay, he will protect you with every resource he has in the World!" the Chief's words held so much weight that each child immediately stood closer to Jay without giving it a second thought.

Chief Danjuma went on to say, "You will go to a place called London. In London you will live and study as normal citizens of Earth. Jay will care for you and protect you as your own fathers would".

Jay wasn't sure how the children would take the news they had just received. He couldn't begin to imagine what they were going through. Jay stepped into their shoes for a moment to visualise how they must feel. He couldn't fathom the emotional distress you must suffer from seeing your home being attacked in such a horrific manner that causes you to lose your parents, families and friends! Then after all that, you're sent to live in a foreign land!

Jay's thought was broken as the eldest of the children looked at him with not one ounce of emotion and said, "Lead the way big man".

This child was 'Raheem'; Raheem was the joint oldest of the children alongside the girl 'Rhiarn'. Raheem and Rhiarn had a striking resemblance to each other and seemed to be siblings. Raheem was straight faced and had an aura that oozed seriousness and intelligence. Even at the tender age of twelve years old you could see he had a lot of maturity, he was clearly the one who the other children would follow.

"GO NOW!" Shouted Santago.

Jay and the children ran towards the plane. The little girl and the last boy instantly took the lead creating a gap of at least 100 metres between them and the rest. The boy and girl reached the plane and waited for Jay and the other children to arrive.

Whilst running towards the plane a soft voice

majestically whispered "Duck bro, duck" into Raheem's mind. As Raheem obeyed this voice and ducked he was struck across his right cheek by one of Bang's killer Panthers who was aiming for his neck.

"Thanks sis, you saved my life again" replied Raheem directly into his sister's mind, it seemed they had a connection which enabled them to communicate telepathically.

As Raheem was distracted by the telepathic conversation, Jay shouted "Nooooooo!" Then shielded Raheem from a monstrous sized Black Lion that was launching an attack on Raheem's blindside. The Black Lion was charging in with its mouth wide open and dripping with saliva, its piercing red eyes were locked on its target... Raheem's neck!

Luckily Jay lifted his right arm just in time to protect Raheem's neck, taking the bite on his own arm and potentially sparing Raheem's life.

Jay struggled and eventually the Lion released its grip, however Jay was injured and had now became the ferocious creature's new target!

Raheem and Jerome managed to shuffle their way out and catch up with the others at the plane.

Jay wasn't as lucky and now he was surrounded by the Black Lion and Bang's soldiers with blood gushing out of his stronger arm and no back up from the Chief and his guards.

Jay looked up and in a distance he could see Santago and the Chief were in the same situation he found himself in, injured and surrounded!

He thought to himself 'I guess this is the end' as he took a deep breath and watched the Black Lion getting ready to launch its attack.

"Let's finish him now!" said one of Bang's soldiers.

"Nar" said another soldier whilst holding his comrade back.

"Lets leave it to him" said Bang's soldier pointing at the blood thirsty Lion.

"He deserves the kill" he said, then Bang's soldiers laughed as they stepped back allowing the Lion to approach Jay.

Jay looked the ferocious Lion dead in its eyes as the beast of a cat powered towards him with its mouth wide open! As the Lion leaped in to bite and rip apart Jay's jugular, amazingly Jay saw the little girl's face flash in the Lion's eyes. Then suddenly the Black Lion changed its course of attack and catapulted its whole body at Bang's soldiers.

Jay thought it was a miracle. He got back up on his feet silently thanking God.

Then Jay made his final steps to the plane and watched the Lion tear through Bang's soldiers.

Jay held the little girl by the hand and said "You did that didn't you, you saved my life".

She replied "Nature, it's what I do," then she smirked with the cutest smile Jay had ever seen.

"What's your name?" said Jay.
"Rhiarn, I'm Raheem's twin sister" she replied with

pride.

"Is it nature that got you to the plane so fast too?" said Jay.

"I guess so, I just thought of a Cheetah... It's the fastest animal on land, so I borrowed its speed" she confidently replied.

Jay grinned and said "I can tell you're from the Tribe of Intelligence and Nature".

"What about you little man, did you use nature to run fast too?" said Jay to the other boy standing there.

"Nar man' I got this speed all the time I don't have to borrow it" he also said with tons of confidence.

"My mum told me I've been blessed with speed and more G'" said the little boy whilst doing a little dance to show off his skills.

"I can see you're gonna' be a problem little man" said Jay in a jokingly manner.

As they all boarded the plane Jay asked the little boy, "What's your name?"

He replied "Danny and I'm from the Tribe of Creativity".

Then Danny shouted "Last one on the plane's a eediot'" and zoomed on to the aircraft.

Everyone followed at their own pace and boarded the private jet.

Chapter 4 - Who Am I?

As Jay and the children sat on the plane, he noticed the cut on Raheem's face. Jay grabbed the plane's first aid kit and began to tend to the cut.

Jay was making a complete mess of it. Raheem looked at him and said

"You don't know what you're doing do you?"

"Not really, I could do with some of that magic water from the mountains" replied Jay.

Raheem asked Jay if he had a phone. Jay thought he may have lost it in the battle, but after giving his pockets a good search he found it and handed it to him. Raheem connected to the jet's Wi-Fi, then went into the phone's internet browser and searched 'How to heal a wound'. Raheem then held his hand on the phone for three seconds flat, as he did this a glow left the phone and travelled into his fingers. Raheem then took over and tended to both his and Jay's wounds with the skill and experience of a seasoned surgeon.

Jay was bewildered! He asked Raheem "How did you do that?"

"There's a lot of things you're gonna' learn about us" replied Raheem who was still a little stand off'ish towards Jay.
"A lot more" cheekily said Rhiarn directly into her twin brother's mind. As she giggled Raheem just about

managed to crack half a smile. Even at a tender young age Raheem seemed to be an extremely serious person.

Just as the plane was about to take off a hand covered in blood smashed against the window.

Jay tensed up and ran to the window with the intention to defend the Chosen Ones, as he approached the window he realised the hand belonged to Chief Danjuma.

Jay shouted out to the pilot "WAIT, STOP THE PLANE!"

Jay ran to the door and was met by the Chief as he opened it.

"Get on the plane Chief, come now" said Jay in an erratic state.

The Chief looked back at Santago who was surrounded by even more of Bang's men and said

"As tempting as that sounds, my work here is not done".

"You're a mad man... it's suicide" said a worried Jay, "Bang's guys keeps coming and coming... there's just too many... it's a madness!"

It was clear to see the Chief was hurt, but he was still confident. He said "Hahahahaha, I've still got a few more tricks up my sleeve. Before you go, you must promise to do one more thing for me"

"Anything Chief, just let me know" replied Jay.

"You showed true honour as you stood side by side with us in battle. I wish this day didn't have to come so soon, but you've made me so proud. I see your mother raised you exactly how we raised her; with honour, strength and intelligence" said Chief Danjuma.

Jay stood confused thinking, 'What does he mean? How does he know my Mum?'

"We must go NOW!" shouted the pilot as he powered back up the engines.

"Tell your mother the way she has raised you is a testament to her excellence. Myself and Jenay are honoured to call her our daughter and feel privileged to be called mother and father by her!"

"WHAT?!?" Screamed Jay as the plane began to take off.

"Close the door and be on your way. Now it's time for you to fulfil your destiny... Grandson!" Shouted Chief Danjuma.

Jay obeyed the Chief's command, but as he locked the aircrafts hatch his mind was completely thrown by the news he had just received.

Jay couldn't help but think, 'mums his daughter?! That makes him my grandfather... and Jenay my grandmother! That makes me a direct descendent of the tribes in Paradise Mountains. No wonder they chose me to come here. It all makes sense now... the invite, the Fire Red Diamond, the instant bond with Jenay... everything!

This journey must have been a test to see if I was ready, but then Bang came? Did Bang know who I really was all this time? Did Bang follow me here? Was Bang's attack my fault? Why don't I have powers? Does my mum have powers?'

A million things ran through Jay's mind in a very short space of time. Eventually he took himself out of his trance with just enough time to see his grandfather jump back into the battle to defend Santago. There was no way the battle could be won, but the Chief and his guards kept fighting like the true warriors they were.

Suddenly it dawned on Jay, as quick as he received grandparents was as quick as he had lost them. Through all the pandemonium Jay managed to catch himself for second. He analysed the situation and took slight comfort in knowing he got to spend time with family that previously didn't even exist to him. Jay realised that after all these years he wasn't alone after all.

As the plane flew higher, he watched Chief Danjuma and Santago battle with Bang's army until they became nothing but a small dot and eventually faded away.

Jay looked over at the children to see they were all asleep, all apart from Raheem who caught eyes with Jay and said "Look at your bag".

Jay looked to see the most astounding glow coming from his bag, it was like an array of rainbows frantically but yet still harmoniously bouncing off each other.

As Jay opened the bag to investigate, a flame started blazing in and outside of his Fire Red Diamond. Then miraculously the other four gemstones jumped out of the bag and began to orbit the Fire Red Diamond.

This left them both speechless, they couldn't do anything but sit and stare at the numerous different colours floating around the plane. The shine was so bright that it woke up the others who were just as speechless as Jay and Raheem.

They all gathered around the gemstones without saying a word, eventually Raheem broke the silence and said "I had my doubts, but Jay you are truly the one".

Jay gently placed the gems back in the bag and told the children "Get some rest. We've got a long journey ahead!"

Chapter 5 - Hiding In Plain Sight

London... 5 Years Later (Present Day)

II If everyone isn't out of this house in fifteen minutes no one's getting lunch money today!" Yelled out Jay. Raheem ran into the room and looked Jay straight in the eyes, then bellowed out "Oi you lot better hurry up, he ain't bluffing!" as he ran around the house like a mad man searching for his other trainer shoe.

Raheem had the ability to read people's emotions and could tell if they were being truthful or telling a lie by just looking in their eyes. This was just one part of the amazing super powers he possessed.

Just over five years had gone by and the children were now teenagers, alot of things had changed. The words from Jay's grandmother constantly played on his mind and he felt it was time to settle down and get married.

Jay rekindled a flame with a lady called Tanya; she was Jay's first love who he met in his local shopping centre on a sunny summer's day. Tanya was creative and intelligent with a perfect dark caramel complexion that complimented and projected her unmissable beauty. Jay saw something special in Tanya from the first day they met, it was truly love at first sight.

Unfortunately their chosen career paths sent them in separate directions. Tanya became a successful tech specialist who created innovative armour and specialist weapons for the Ministry of Defence (MOD). She did this job for years and was very successful in her field, however she also had a passion for fashion which led her to come back to London and pursue her dream of becoming a high end designer.

A few years down the line Jay and Tanya randomly reconnected at a charity event. Since that day they have been inseparable. Jay and Tanya tied the knot and legally adopted the four children, growing them as their own.

Jay and Tanya taught the children the importance of hiding their super powers, this was especially harder when they were young children as it was difficult to explain to them the different rules of the World they now lived in. Initially the children couldn't comprehend that their abilities weren't accepted in this new land and that it could place them in harms way. The children came from Paradise Mountains – a place where super powers weren't looked at as super - in fact what we call super powers was something as normal as breathing to them.

A few years back, Jay had some friends round his home for a BBQ party to celebrate Jay and Tanya's engagement. The friends brought their offsprings along to play with Jay's new children. Whilst the adults were out in the garden having a drink and lighting the coal, the children became peckish and wanted a snack. With all the adults preoccupied and engrossed in conversation the kids struggled to get their attention to ask for permission to have some biscuits, so Rhiarn decided to take the matter into her own hands! Rhiarn summoned the powers of a Canary, then she flew up to the top shelf and grabbed the Biscuit tin. All the children were stunned and amazed! They couldn't believe what they witnessed. They ran outside and interrupted the adults to tell them how a bird appeared in Rhiarn's eyes then she flew up as high as the ceiling and grabbed the Biscuit tin. Jay and Tanya stood nervous and worried thinking that everyone would now realise the children have super powers. They didn't know how they were going to get out of this one! Then luckily one of Jay's friends laughed and shouted out, "What's wrong with these kids, they got too much imagination". All the other adults busted out laughing and told the children to go back inside and continue to play.

"That was mad close" whispered Jay to Tanya.

From that day Jay realised that he had a major task ahead of him. Hiding the powers and true identities of the children would be hard work! However, Jay also had a soft spot and sympathised with the children as they were only kids. He felt it was a little unfair to force them to lie about who they are and where they're from. How can you punish a child for speaking the truth? But there were big things at stake, potentially the whole World! So Jay had to make the hard call and trained the children to hide their past and live life under new identities.

However Jay felt it would be wrong to completely change their whole identity and unintentionally lead them to lose their culture. So Jay kept their real names and every night he ensured he told them stories of Paradise Mountains so they would never forget who they are!

From a young age the children were all trained in Mixed Martial Arts (MMA), this not only gave them amazing fighting skills but this also added to their discipline and honour.

As time went by they all grew into typical 'London' teenagers who embraced the street culture through fashion and music. Being the children of a millionaire couple came with its perks, they were always sporting the latest tracksuits and designer gear whilst partying and listening to the latest songs from the Grime and UK Rap scene.

Rhiarn really looked up to Tanya and this made her grow into a real fashionista! She was known to set new fashion trends and was well respected by all her peers. She was loved by the 'Cool Kids' and the so called 'Geeks' alike.

Being from the Tribe of Nature, Rhiarn and Raheem had super intelligence which enabled them to excel academically, they were so far advanced that often they would have to purposely make mistakes in tests and homework in order to protect their secret abilities. This would sometimes frustrate Raheem, he had a serious nature and didn't like to play about! Raheem couldn't see why he should belittle himself in any way; he was full of pride. Rhiarn was more laid back and even though she too had great pride in her abilities and where she was from, she understood the importance of 'playing the fool' at times to protect the greater good.

Rhiarn also had the ability to draw the power from any animal in the World she could think of, great or small. As she grew older she learnt how to use these powers in an effective manner.

Raheem was the natural leader amongst the children, he was the big brother to all of them and the go to guy if any of them had problems. He was very protective of his family and would put it all on the line for them at any given time. It was only in regards to his family when Raheem would act purely out of emotion and not from his strategic brain. His super powers quickly began to advance to a new level, he not only could read someone's emotions and see if they was telling the truth or not, he could also touch someone and receive all the knowledge he request from that person's brain.

Danny fitted right into London and became one of the most popular teens in the area. He excelled in sports and was in every school sports team he chose to be in. Danny had now developed into what was known as a 'Speed Prince' which was the title given to a young male with super speed in Paradise Mountains. This was the usual way that the super powers advanced for people from his tribe, the next level for him to achieve would be a 'Speed King'. Although he wasn't very academic he managed to adequately get through school due to his charm and charisma. Danny would often get in trouble with Jay for finding the easy way out of school tasks, like having girls do his homework. Danny was a natural born charmer who knew how to use his charisma to get what he wanted in life.

Unfortunately not all the children had the same positive experience, Jerome didn't find it so easy to fit in.

Jerome became unstoppably strong! He stood at a

small 5ft 5" but he had a strength that this World had never seen before. He was indestructible with unmeasurable power.

Jerome didn't really like living in London. After leaving Paradise Mountains he never really had any one he could play with in the way he could play when he was amongst his tribe. Jerome was a typical little boy, he loved to play rough and play fight, however this was a problem due to the strength he possessed. All the other children in the area couldn't match an ounce of his power so when they played with Jerome they would often leave injured. Children became too scared to play with him leading him to feel left out and alone. Rhiarn would sympathise with him and often draw the strength of Gorillas and Rhinos to give her little brother an opportunity to play. This would work in his younger years, but as he got older he became way too strong for her too!

Jerome often felt like the odd one out. This would upset him and eventually make him react. Jay tried to find many ways to deal with his anger and frustrations, which often didn't work. Then one day Jay noticed Jerome grew a love for music. Rap music in particular became a major part of Jerome's life, when he felt stressed or upset he would listen to some to calm down.

Jerome then got into writing raps and began to use it as a way to vent.

Chapter 6 - It Goes Down At StackTown!

The children were all dressed and ready for school, Jay gave them their lunch money and sent them on their way. They all attend the same school - London Academy. London Academy is a public secondary school with sixth form that was only a short ten minute walk away from their home. Even though he could afford it, Jay refused to send the children to a private school as he wanted them to experience life in London to the fullest. Every morning they would walk to school together but unfortunately being in different academic years meant their timetables weren't in sync, so after school they all made their own separate ways home.

In the local area there was a chicken and chip shop called StackTown. It was a place where everyone would go after school to just chill and eat food. Boys from the area would try to show off and look cool to get the girls' attention and the girls would act like they weren't paying the boys no mind whilst secretly sitting in their groups crushing on the boys they like.

For years people went StackTown to just chill and link up. They would also hold dance competitions, open mic events and talent shows for the local teenagers. It was a cool and safe place to be. Unfortunately things at StackTown changed since last summer! When evening struck the local gang "Da Grabberz" would hang around outside and cause trouble doing petty theft and robberies, just being a general nuisance.

When Jay heard of all the trouble that was taking place down there he gave the children strict instructions, telling them they must be home by 5pm to avoid any possible trouble. Jerome was upset by this as StackTown was the only thing he liked in London. It was his favourite place to go and now Da Grabberz had effectively took this away from him. Da Grabberz sensed that Jerome had a bad vibe towards them and although a few of them were friends with Danny, they still made it clear that they didn't like Jerome either!

It was a normal Wednesday, everyone was at school and all was well.

Jerome was happy as there was an open mic and under 18's rave at StackTown this coming Saturday. Jay didn't allow the teens to attend raves too much as they were usually magnets for trouble, but as Jay's friend owned StackTown he gave them permission to go... as long as they were well behaved at school.

Jerome's day went well until his last period where he got a detention for talking back to his teacher in class. He was upset because he didn't think he was in the wrong. His friend whispered a joke to him and when he laughed the teacher turned around and told him off. When he tried to explain himself to the teacher he was kicked out of class for back chatting. Jerome was upset as he wanted to get down to StackTown straight after school and put his name on the list for the open mic session before the deadline.

As soon as he was released from detention Jerome ran straight to StackTown. By time he arrived it was late and Da Grabberz were already outside the food spot causing trouble. As Jerome reached the front of the shop he noticed three Grabberz were blocking the entrance.

"Sorry bro, I need to get through" said Jerome in a polite tone trying to avoid confrontation.

"Yeah well wait, can't you see I'm talking" replied one of the Grabberz.

"Bro, you're blocking the entrance to a shop...move your conversation over there ennit!" said Jerome with his faced screwed up.

"This little boy thinks he's bad" laughed the Grabber. Then he went on to say "Don't let me embarrass you out 'ere G'".

"I would love you to try it, don't be fooled by my size... I'm active bro!" replied Jerome whilst walking over to the Grabber with his hands out. Jerome wanted the opportunity to put him in his place and release all his frustrations.

They got face to face and another Grabber jumped up and intervened saying "Louw' him gang, that's Danny's little brother" trying to defuse the situation.

"You're lucky" said the Grabber, "but I'm letting you know if I see you again and you try act bad or even look at me funny, I'm gonna' punch you up... Danny's brother or not!"

"Am I meant to be shook? Hahaha I'm begging you please, do it and make my day you fool!" said Jerome as he walked through and put his name on the list just before the deadline.

When Jerome got home lucky for him Jay had left on an overnight business trip, meaning Jay didn't find out about his detention.

Danny received a text about his brother's argument at StackTown.

"What happened with you and Da Grabberz bro?" Asked Danny.

"Arrr nothing one of them tried to pattern man, he's lucky I didn't smash his face in!" replied Jerome.

"Don't worry bro they can't do you nothing hahahaha, I've squashed it anyway" said Danny.

Raheem overheard the conversation from the other room, he angrily burst into the room shouting "Who tried to trouble my little bro, I swear down I'll rip up every one of them Grabberz you know... let me know if any of them carry it on!"

Jerome laughed, he found it funny that everyone wanted to defend him even though he was the strongest in the room.

Even Rhiarn made her remarks stating "That Grabber yout' is cute, but if he messes with my brother it's a mad ting'... watch I'mma' make Chanel dump him!"

Jerome assured them all that he had it under control.

It was now Thursday, the word of the argument was ringing around the school. Everyone was talking about it, people even started making up their own versions of the minor altercation, chinese whispers was in full affect. Jerome heard stories reporting that he was beat up by Da Grabberz and in contrary he also heard stories that he embarrassed one of the main Grabbers and sent him home crying.

Jerome was getting a new respect,in school, but honestly he didn't like it. He knew this would have a knock on effect, he was fully aware that Da Grabberz would want to settle the score and prove to everyone that they were the baddest in school and the whole ends'. It was all getting to him, he didn't like the fact that people were talking about him and spreading lies at that.

As Jerome predicted, there were now rumours that Da Grabberz wanted to move to him after school! Unfortunately for Da Grabberz they didn't know they'd picked a fight with one of the strongest people in the World.

Jerome tried to keep calm remembering that if he got in trouble he would not be allowed to go to the open mic rave on Saturday, but this was going to be a hard task as Jerome was naturally hot headed and whenever there was a threat his natural instinct was to defend with attack straight away!

Third period was just before lunch, it was Science. Jerome already hated this subject and found it hard to concentrate in this lesson, but this whole situation made it even worse. He deliberated with himself enduring a solo mental battle through the whole period, he didn't manage to get one bit of his work done!

Then just before the pips went off to signal the end of the lesson he clenched his fist and decided that he was going to confront Da Grabberz NOW!.

As soon as the pips sounded Jerome jumped up raring to go and look for Da Grabberz so he can let them have it! In the back of his mind he could hear Jay's voice saying "You have nothing to prove, no one in this city can match your strength! Fighting them will only put your identity at risk".

Jerome knew the words that rang in his mind were correct, but he couldn't ignore what was going on. With all this adding to the frustrations he was constantly bottling up, he had reached his final straw.

Jerome told himself 'I'll go real easy on them, that way I won't give up my identity but I can put them in their place. It's a win win situation!' convincing himself that he was doing the right thing.

Jerome ran towards the football pen where he knew Da Grabberz would be congregating.

Jerome saw the main culprit, he was surrounded by at least six friends and a bunch of random school pupils who were just playing and doing their thing.

Jerome aggressively ran up and confronted him...

"So what you saying now gang, why you been talking rubbish?"

The Grabber laughed saying "This little fool don't quit. You're brave bro I'll give you that, but you better shut your mout' before you get hurt" as he turned back to the conversation.

Jerome responded, "You're always talking, but that's

all it is... talk!"

Feeling that he was not being taken serious, Jerome took a football that rolled by and threw it at the Grabber's back.

The Grabber spun round enraged and punched Jerome in his face. It was a loud SMACKKKKK! Everyone shouted "Oooouuuuhhh".

A crowd started to gather.

Unphased by the punch, Jerome laughed and said "Thank you".

This was perfect as all Jerome wanted was for the Grabber to hit him first, because he firmly believed that if the other person strikes first he wouldn't be in trouble with Jay, as Jay always taught them to defend themselves.

To the surprise of everyone there, Jerome jumped up and gave the Grabber a thunderous right hook to the face sending him flying across the football pen. Another Grabber came running towards Jerome to defend his fellow gang member. He swung a punch at Jerome, but Jerome ducked the blow then grabbed him by his collar and gave him a stiff knee to his gut followed by a throw that launched him at least five metres across the pitch.

With one Grabber knocked out cold and the other one folded, the remaining Grabberz were now scared stiff.

Jerome looked at them and said "So who's the strongest Grabber here? I dare you to step forward so I can batter you too!"

They all looked away scared, well... all except one who

was sneaking up behind Jerome with a glass bottle! The Grabber got right behind Jerome without him noticing, then with the bottle clenched tight in his fist he drew back his hand and was ready to shut Jerome up good and proper! The Grabber was about one inch away from viciously making the bottle smash into the back of Jerome's head... then literally out of nowhere Danny came running in with a double combo kick that swiftly kicked the bottle out of the Grabberz hand before it could connect with Jerome, before the Grabber could even think what was going on, Danny's heel clobbered into the his jaw knocking the Grabber spark out.

A teacher came and dragged Jerome and Danny away. Everyone in the playground went ballistic! Cheering and shouting in disbelief, Jerome was the man! He won a fight with some of the most infamous gang members in the school.

Releasing his tension on the Grabberz didn't feel as good as Jerome anticipated it to be. He didn't feel content at all, instead he had a strange feeling of guilt. Jerome realised he went against everything Jay taught him and knew his actions will disappointment Jay, Tanya and maybe even his siblings.

Just after Jay flew back in from his business trip he received a call from the school stating that Danny and Jerome have been sent home on a three day suspension for a fight which left one boy with a broken jaw and another with mild concussion. The teacher gave Jay a full rundown of the story including today's fight and the altercation outside StackTown the day before. They even told him about the after school detention.

Jay was furious! The airport was a two hour drive away, he told his trusted driver to floor it and take him straight home! Jay's two hour trip was cut down by half an hour as his driver could see the anger in his eyes.

Jerome and Danny were at home panicking trying to come up with a story to tell Jay. They even went as far as asking Tanya to conspire with them! Rhiarn kept on winding them up laughing saying that Jay was going to punish them so hard! She found the situation funny, however Raheem was not amused at all. Raheem vowed to destroy each of the Grabberz for troubling his little brother. Raheem was a rational thinker who could always pick the smartest strategy in any situation, but when it involved his family or what he loved he took no prisoners and the only solution in his mind was to go to war; no retreat no surrender!

BOOOOMMMMM, the front door swung open then slammed shut!

"Jerome... Danny... Get in Here... NOW!" shouted Jay.

Jerome took a big gulp and Danny took a deep breath then they slowly walked down the stairs to meet Jay.

"Oh now you're moving slow yeah Danny?! One of you better tell me what happened at school!" Demanded Jay.

Jerome began to tell the story that him and Danny conspired.

"What happened was, me and Danny was just going to get lunch..."

Jay cut Jerome's words short and said "Don't you dare

lie to me about going to get lunch... your teachers told me everything!"

"So why d'you want us to tell you, if you already know fam?" said a cocky Danny as he kissed his teeth. Danny was cheeky and had an answer for everything.

"Right now ain't the time for your lip Danny" said a serious Jay.

"Sorry Jay" apologised Danny as he looked at the ground.

Jerome and Danny went on to explain the situation and how it took place. Jay started to calm down a bit as he realised Jerome was technically defending himself and Danny was just defending Jerome.

However Jay was still angry that Jerome went looking for the Grabberz.

"What have I always told you, if you go looking for trouble... trouble will find you!" Said Jay.

"You may have won this fight against a bunch of school kids, but one day you might get into some real beef and that kind of stupid behaviour can get you killed!"

"You should know better, I've taught you better than this! There is nothing to gain from fighting people you are literally a million times stronger than!" explained Jay.

Even though Jay calmed down a little, his anger shot right back up when it dawned on him that the boys could have exposed their powers!

Jay went crazy, shouting "YOU IDIOTS, you could've

showed the whole school your powers! You should be ashamed of yourselves. You're gonna have everybody walking and thinking you're little freaks!"

"IS THAT WHAT YOU THINK OF US!" shouted back Jerome.

Jerome had enough, he already felt restricted and out of place ever since he came to London. Jay words were the only thing he took comfort in, so hearing this led to him having an outburst screaming, "Little freaks... that's all we are to you! All you ever do is restrict us and not allow us to be who we are! I hate it here in London and I hate you!" Jerome then stamped off to his room slamming his door shut so hard that the whole floor shook.

Everyone in the house was shell shocked and didn't know how to react.

"Everyone get out of my face!" Demanded Jay.

All the teens retired to their rooms for the night.

On the way out, Raheem walked over to Jay to assure him "Don't worry, I could see in his eyes he didn't mean it... he's just a bit confused."

"I've tried to do my best for you all" said Jay.

"We know this" replied Raheem then he went on to say "but it's been hard for us to settle in this new land, especially Jerome. Give him some time he'll be cool by tomorrow" then he hugged Jay and walked to his room.

That night Jay sat and thought about everything. As he layed down resting his head in Tanya's arms he asked her "Am I being too harsh? What's the worst that can happen if I let them use their powers?" Without given her a chance to answer, he went on to say "On the other hand them exposing themselves can put them and whatever's left of Paradise Mountains at risk... if anything's left of Paradise Mountains. I don't know what to do, maybe I've bitten of more than I can chew babes" Jay was doubting his ability to protect and grow the Chosen Children.

Tanya gently ran her hand through Jay's hair and told him "Heavy is the head that wears the crown, nobody said this would be easy Jay. Sleep on it and tomorrow I'm sure everything will be cool".

Jay kissed Tanya and then closed his eyes whilst thinking, 'I need to figure out a way to make this better for everyone' as he fell asleep with a heavy mind and a torn heart, wanting the best for his family.

Chapter 6.5 - Out of hiding!

Jay finally managed to get a good night's sleep. First thing in the morning he decided to call his mum. Besides Tanya, Jay's mother was the only other person who knew who the children really were. He rang her and told her his situation, he explained that one half of him wanted the teens to embrace their powers and skills but the other half of him wanted to allow them to be teenagers and live normal lives.

"Son, you were chosen for a reason. You may not see how much wisdom you possess as you're directly walking through the trials and tribulations, but prophecy wouldn't have trusted you with this task if it wasn't 100% sure of your capabilities... make a decision" said Mummy G.

She then added "I will say one thing though, these are not normal teenagers. According to prophecy, they are the ones who will save the World so maybe you should treat them abit more accordingly."

Jay's mind was much clearer after he spoke with his mother, so clear that he was confident enough to make the major decision to allow the children to use their powers. He created a plan to boost their training to ensure they could control the powers they had been gifted with.

Jay thought if we're going to do this, we're going to do it properly! He went over to his safe, put in his combination and took out the five gemstones he was given in the Paradise Mountains. Jay took these gemstones to his trusted jeweller with the intention of creating five special necklaces coupled with unique platinum pendant casings that can hold the gems.

Jay got home and called Tanya into their bedroom.
"Fancy making something special babes?"
Knowing exactly what was on Jay's mind, Tanya Smiled at him and said
"I've been waiting for you to ask"

"Basically I thought you know what... we should let them be what they're destined to be, I even got a name for them... Squad Gigantic, what d'you think?" Said Jay

"Yeah Squad Gigantic... SG, i love it! Sounds like real super heroes" replied Tanya

"Yep that's what I thought, but big and serious babes... what are super heroes without the baddest suits?" Said Jay.

"You tell me hun" replied Tanya as she smiled again.

Tanya was so happy that Jay was embracing the teens' super powers that she wrapped her arms around him saying "I knew you would make the right decision".

Jay knew Tanya was the perfect person for the job, her fashion design skills alongside her tech knowledge made her the ideal candidate for making the teens suits.

Tanya began to brainstorm outfit designs for the squad's uniforms. She aimed to create something that was not only trendy and cool, but also bespoke enough to match each members' individual powers and needs. Something that dealt with the physics of Danny's speed without burning away, whilst still being flexible and comfortable enough for the rest to fight freely when defending themselves against ruthless enemies.

Tanya shooed Jay out of the house and got straight to work on the outfits.

Later that day Jay had a heart to heart talk with Jerome, he wanted to clear the air and find out his son's true feelings.

Jerome apologised for the outburst and took back everything he said. He wanted Jay to know that he loved him and that he and the others saw him as their father. Jay also apologised for making comments that hurt Jerome's feelings. He explained that he was also new to the world of fatherhood and that he makes mistakes just like everyone else. However, Jay still said Jerome was going to be punished for the fight and not following rules.

"I'm glad we've had this heart to heart and you know I love you and all that... but you still ain't going anywhere on Saturday! I don't care if you had bars to bun' the whole place down or whatever you call it. The only place you're spitting bars is in your room this weekend" said Jay as he walked out Jerome's room.

Jerome laughed and accepted the punishment!

Chapter 7 - Squad Gigantic!

A good few weeks had passed without any problems or issues, things seemed to be back to normal in the Gigantic household. Da Grabberz weren't happy with Jerome and Danny, but they knew better than to create any new situations.

Tanya called on some of her MOD contacts, a secret construction team who specialise in building state of the art headquarters and training camps for agents. Following Tanya's blueprints and plans, the team built a hidden HQ and training camp in the basement which ran under the grounds of the Gigantic's mansion.

The HQ was Tanya's brain child, since the first day she discovered the children's powers she began sketching it out in her mind, knowing the day will eventually come when a HQ would be needed.

The HQ consisted of sophisticated technology with the aim of advancing the teens skills. There was also a fully equipped workshop for Tanya to create new tech and systems to support the teens. Training wise, not only is there a top of the range MMA Gym with all the extras, there's also bespoke training units designed and developed to cater to each person's individual needs.

Danny's section was a special speed track tunnel named the 'Velocitizer'. The Velocitizer began and ended at the mansion's grounds, but ran underneath parts of the city. It has a one mile track that had been assembled inside a purpose built cloaked tunnel which isn't visible to the human eye. The Velocitizer was powered by Tanya's operating system, its main objective was to develop Danny's speed and velocity whilst monitoring his vitals and accurately recording his development. The Velocitizer was also armed with high calibre machine guns that fired high speed rubber bullets and rocket launchers that released blank heat seeking missiles to constantly challenge Danny during unique simulation scenarios that the Velocitizer created.

The team also built a unit called the 'Nature Corner' for Rhiarn. This area integrates virtual reality with real life allowing Rhiarn to battle and train with all elements of nature known to man. A simple press of a button could have Rhiarn fighting her way out of an erupting volcano or wrestling with a polar bear in the North Pole. This built her ability to be at one with nature and learn new ways to tackle tasks whilst broadening her horizons on which elements and animals to draw power from.

Apart from top neuro technology and a fully loaded digital library to constantly gain knowledge from, Truth didn't need much. His training regime consisted of good old hard work and grit, he was relentless in the gym as well as the MMA mats and Octagon.

The last area was named 'The Bruck Down'. This area was built with Jerome in mind. It's filled with some of the most durable, toughest and hardest materials in the World such as concrete slabs reinforced with carbon composite and a metallic chemical element called Osmium; it even had maraging steel pillars. These nearly indestructible items were basically put in the Bruck Down just for Jerome to use as Punching bags. This area also has sensors that connect to a monitoring system that Tanya called the Mega Dynamometer, also known as the Mega D. The sensors sent messages to the Mega D to record growth in Jerome's power and strength.

The Mega Dynamometer, Velocitizer and the Nature Corner are all connected to Tanya's mainframe system in the new HQ.

Tanya built this system to her very own spec. Not only does it control the whole of HQ and the squad's training, it was also the mother computer that led all operations for the squad. This system had the power to do nearly anything! From giving Tanya access to satellites in space and CCTV all over the World, to intercepting any other operating system on the entire planet... and probably beyond! This system was built to play a vital role in protecting the teens whilst they're out on missions.

Tanya embedded a Micro Personal Digital Assistant (PDA) system to each suits watch and mask piece. This enabled the teens to be connected to her complex system at any given time, so no matter where in the world the teens were, they would never be alone.

It was Saturday morning and Jay received a phone call from his jeweller. Incredibly all his items were ready a whole week before the deadline.

Jay and Tanya told the children they were having a family night in as they had something important to tell everyone. The teens were excited because family night meant BBQ and games. BBQ was the favourite style of cuisine in the Gigantic household. They would cook up Beef Short Ribs and BBQ Chicken Quarters then serve them with Tanya's famous Snapz, Saltfish Fritters, Potato Salad and Coleslaw!

Jay went and collected the necklaces he had made up. Each necklace was identical, they were made out of platinum and hand finished in a one of a kind angled twist link. Each necklace also had a solid platinum pendant space for each teen's gem to effortlessly slot in and out.

When everyone finished stuffing their faces, Jay presented the necklaces on the dining table. The exquisitely designed jewellery immediately caught the teenagers' eyes and everyone rushed towards them.

"What you doing man, wait? Who said they were yours?" joked Jay. As much as Jay tried he couldn't fool them, they knew the necklaces belonged to them.

Jay confessed and said "They are yours but calm down. Let me explain why you're getting them, it's much more than a gift!"

The room fell silent.

"These come with a lot of responsibility" said Jay with a now stern face.

Jay saw this moment as the perfect time to explain to the children what the gemstones were and why they're so important to each one of them. "These gemstones are the key to your powers. In Paradise Mountains children are born daily and each and every one of them are special. However when a child of prophecy is born its extra special as a unique gemstone also rises within twenty four hours of the birth. This gemstone surfaces underneath wherever the baby first lays it head. This is an honour that the people of the Paradise Mountains wish for, as this means your child is amongst the chosen ones who only come every so often with the destiny to protect and lead Earth" explained Jay.

The children sat and listened in awe, all but Danny who couldn't help himself but to laugh out loud and say "You know it's something serious cos' Jay's putting on that fake 'Chief' voice that he uses when he wants to sound smart".

"Danny shut up, now ain't the time for your jokes bro" said Raheem.

Jay gave Danny a piercing look then cut his eyes at him as he looked back at the rest and continued to speak. As Jay spoke, the gemstones began to glow and rise in the exact same way they rose when they were on the plane leaving Paradise Mountains.
As the gems shot colours around the room Jay stated "Each of your gemstones are connected to your individual powers... if you lose your gemstone your powers will be replicated into the soul of the person who possesses them! If this happens to be hands of evil... the whole World as we know it will be at risk! God forbid an evil being gets hold of all these gemstones, because the gemstones powers will combine and make that person unstoppable! You must protect these gems with your life!"

Tanya then added "Although these necklaces are not from the Paradise Mountains, they play a vital role in being the conductor that will draw further energy from your gemstones... so you must also guard the necklaces with extreme caution".

Jay and Tanya called the teens over to receive their necklaces and gems.

"Raheem and Rhiarn come up first, these are your precious pieces" said Tanya
Then Jay took over.
"Raheem you have the 'Purple Star Diamond' and Rhiarn you have the 'Pink Star Diamond', two of the rarest gemstones in the World. You're both extra special as the Paradise Mountains had never seen a set of twins receive the gemstones. On the night of your birth two gemstones appeared, one under each cot you both slept in.
The following morning the whole of Paradise Mountains came together and celebrated the birth of the 'Chosen Twins' with a big feast followed by entertainment. It was a joyous occasion that brought a new hope for the future."
As expected Raheem showed little emotion, but Jay knew he was touched by the manner he approached and hugged him as he received the necklace and Purple Star Diamond. Rhiarn was full of pride, she put hers on straight away and true to her fashionista style, she adjusted her hair to match her new jewellery.

"Jerome this is your gemstone, Orange Painite. You actually had the strength to rip your gem out of the rocks surface as it appeared" explained Jay. "Why does that not surprise me?" laughed out Danny
"Shut your mout' rudeboy!" replied Jerome whilst everyone laughed.

"Yeah, shut up Danny!" instructed Jay as he brought order back to the room.

"The Orange Painite is one of the World's strongest gems. This represents your power and strength... big man ting'... you better guard this with all you got" said Jay.

"I will Jay, I will" said a sincere Jerome.

"I mean it, this ain't a toy or game! I need you to take this serious. Today's the day you become a man!" said Jay, being extra clear and slightly harsh as Jerome is the youngest member of the family.

Before Jerome could even take his necklace and gemstone properly Danny jumped up and ran towards Jay.

"Move man" said Jerome and effortlessly pushed Danny out of his path.

"Alright bro... watch" said Danny, playfully threatening his younger brother as he got back on his feet. Jay just laughed. Danny and Jerome had a typical brotherly love hate relationship and always liked to wind each other up. Even though they would probably disagree, it was clear to see that they had an extremely tight bond.

"Last but definitely not least, here's your gemstone Danny. It's a Golden Beryl" said Jay.

"That some chick ting" laughed Jerome, getting his own back for the comment Danny made earlier.

Danny didn't care what Jerome had to say, he had the biggest smile on his face but it wasn't because of how special the moment was. It was simply because he had always begged Jay for a chain as all the older guys who were rated in the area had one and Danny wanted to be the man just like them.

"It looks better than your dead orange stone G" replied Danny.
"You're a fool, this is that real G' colour bro. What's Golden Beryl? That's some flower man ting" said Jerome as he rolled around laughing.

"You lot stop your foolishness, this is serious" said Raheem, regulating his younger brothers.

"Danny, let me make this clear. This isn't no fashion accessory or anything that's meant to make you look like a bad boy or... 'that guy'. This is an important part of your culture and the World literally depends on it! DO NOT MESS ABOUT with it, you hear me?" said Jay.

"This goes out to all of you, your blood mother and fathers fought with their lives to protect you and these gems. You better make sure they didn't give their all in vein!" said Tanya in a firm voice!

Tanya often had a gentle approach to things but when she spoke in a firm tone, everyone knew to listen. That statement from Tanya brought an instant calm back to the room. Even though they loved Jay and Tanya dearly, each teenager really missed their parents and still had a big gap in their hearts for them that could never be filled.

"I get you big man, don't worry I fully understand the importance. I won't let no one finesse me for it, trust!" said Danny as serious as he gets.

Jay decided to lighten the mood once again and took out his own necklace.

"You know I weren't getting left out, I might not have the powers but my Fire Red Diamond is still the big ting" laughed Jay.

Raheem looked Jay dead in his eyes and said "Hold on… we're allowed to use our powers?"

Jay paused for a second, then with the happiest expression on his face, he looked at each teenager and said

"Yep! Get ready to be super heroes!"

They all jumped up out of happiness, even Raheem! Jay knew how much this meant to them, it was the freedom they had wanted ever since they moved to London.

"Don't get too excited though, there's still gonna' be rules. Powers are only to be used for good! There's gonna be intensive training with harsh discipline and most importantly… your identities must be protected at all times! So no one else in this World is to know about this" said Jay.

"100! We totally understand" said Rhiarn as all her brothers also agreed.

The teens were so excited they totally forgot about everything that was going on around them. They started to discuss which one of the Grabberz they wanted to go for first and how much they were going to improve the city.

The room was chaotic. The teens were all about to leave then Tanya stopped them and said "Wait there's more, grab your necklaces and gems... lets go down to the basement". Tanya and Jay led the way.

They arrived at the basement and Tanya stood in front of what looked like a standard hard wood door. She stood still for three seconds, then a fluorescent blue laser beam came out of nowhere and scanned her retina. The beam then proceeded to scan everyone else's retinas too.

A voice appeared and identified Tanya by saying "Yooo Tanny Tan Tan, what's goin'? I see you got the full squad with you today... I hope everyone's calm still".

The basic basement door disappeared! It was nothing but a hologram used to deceive the naked eye and cover the real entrance to their new high spec HQ. As the hologram disappeared, a circular blast door with a logo which looked an emblem with SG embedded in the centre slowly dilated and they all walked in.

"MAD MAAD MAAAAADDDD!" said Danny.

"What's this?" said Rhiarn.

"I knew you guys were up to something" said Raheem.

"All this time I thought Jay was building a new games room or sutum' down 'ere, you lot are snakes" said Jerome.

"I'll let Tanya explain" said Jay.

"This is our new HQ, this is where we're gonna' operate from and... save the World" laughed Tanya.

The teens couldn't believe their eyes. Tanya went on to

show them the training areas, explaining all its purposes and how everything works. The teens' instincts naturally took them to their designated training areas where they all instantaneously began to use the equipment. Jay called them and brought back order within the HQ.

"They'll be plenty of time for all that, trust me. I'm gonna' have you lot in here until you hate it!" joked Jay. "I doubt that mate, I don't think I could ever get bored in here" replied Danny.
"Hush and be quiet anyway, I still got one more thing to show you" said Tanya.

Tanya walked over to the centre of the HQ and said "Raise the SG System". The same voice from the door returned and said "Say nut'um', SG System elevating".

"Rah' what's that?" said Raheem as the SG System emerged out of the ground. He was in love with the machines complexity.
"This is the SG System. It's the hub of everything you see here and everything we're about to do. This isn't what I wanted to show you though" said Tanya as she stood next to Raheem.
"Raheem, you see that button there, second to the left… press it" instructed Tanya.
Raheem located the button and pressed it. As soon as he pressed the button, five large capsules slowly emerged from the ground.

"What the.....?" said Jerome.
Jay smiled and said "I know exactly what that is… how you gonna' be super heroes without suits?"

"NO WAYYY!" shouted Danny whilst Rhiarn screamed! The teens were ecstatic, they ran up to the capsules and lost their minds.

The suits were perfect. The colour scheme was black with touches of chrome, then each suit was finished off with each teens' individual gemstone colours running through it. They were truly something else, it was obvious no detail was spared and each suit was completed to a high quality finish.
Every suit had a SG emblem on the right arm. There was also a special compartment on the neck that led to the chest, this was where the necklace locked into. Just beneath this area there was a centre piece where the pendant and teens' gemstones slotted into perfectly. The suits also had half face masks to protect the teens' identities. These mask cleverly had hologram screens built in which projected real time information that may need to be streamed to their PDA's from the SG System, this enabled each member to communicate with Tanya and each other at all times.

Once the gemstone is slotted into the centre piece of the SG Suit, the PDA and electronic systems activate by drawing power from the gemstone which is conducted through the platinum necklace. The PDA and electronic systems allow Tanya and Jay to monitor any damaged sustained to the teens, track their whereabouts and remotely send strategies and instructions directly to each person. The suits were amazing, even greater than what Jay imagined.

Danny left the pandemonium for a second and counted the capsules that contained the suits. Then he turned around and counted his siblings.

"Why's there five capsules, ain't there only four of us?" said Danny in confusion.
"There's no way I was getting left out mate" replied Jay.

They all laughed knowing that Jay had a childish element to his character.
There was no way Jay would miss the opportunity to have his very own super hero suit. Jay's suit wasn't exactly the same as the others, in fact the upper piece was more the size of a T-shirt, but nevertheless it possessed the same attributes that the full suits possessed.

"You sure there isn't something you're not telling us big man?" inquisitively implied Rhiarn, thinking Jay may be hiding some sort of super powers from the family.
"I wish luv'" replied Jay.

Jay would've loved to have had super powers. This was something that always played on his mind. He couldn't make sense of it all, he never understood why and how he could be prophesied to lead the Chosen Ones and have the Fire Red Diamond, but still have no super powers. He was forever thinking 'my grandfather is Chief Danjuma. I must've inherited something!' I guess it just wasn't Jay's fate, however his destiny was to grow and protect the special children and deep down inside he was good with that.

"Let's look at these suits" said Jay as he snapped out of his feelings.

The capsule doors opened and released a cold smoke, for the first time ever everyone was able to touch and feel their suits.

Each suit was made out of a unique material that Tanya developed when she was on a job for the MOD. She named the material Graphex!

Graphex is comprised from a complex mix of a few materials. Firstly a material called Nomex which stands well against heat, chemicals and radiation is combined with extremely thin and light layers of cut down Polycarbonate sheets. This combination is then integrated with a metal called Graphite which boasts of being as thin as paper, but as strong as steel. The Graphex is then intricately mixed with elasticated silk, this allows the squad to manoeuvre freely and use their powers in a waterproof suit that can protect them from enemy onslaughts of bullets and even explosions.

Tanya got back everyone's attention and said "Put on your necklaces". Whilst they all did as instructed, Tanya gave each person a watch.

"You giving us Roleys'" shouted out Danny in joy.

Tanya laughed and said "Not quite Danny, these are the SG Watches... it may look like a Roley', but trust me they're not that!"

"What you saying they're fake! I ain't wearing no fake ting'... bad man don't do that!" Said Danny "Just shut your mout' and listen!" Shouted Raheem putting an end to Danny's talking.

Tanya took back lead of the conversation and said "As I was saying, put them on your left wrist and press the button on the crown winder three times".

The watches were amazing, as they pressed the crown winder each watches appearance changed from a Roley' to a much more modern metallic cuff style watch which was at least five times bigger than the initial Roley' design and also had a full colour screen.
In its actual form the SG Watches we're a lot more bulky than an average everyday watch, so it was likely to cause too much attention. To overcome this potential issue Tanya created a cloak reflection that hid the watch from the natural eye and reflected back an image of a Roley' wrist watch.

Everyone was so excited and intrigued by the transition that they stood in awe awaiting Tanya's next words.
As they awaited instruction the screen on the teens watches changed to a thumb print scanner, Tanya told the teens to place their thumbs on the scanners, as they did this the watches flashed green indicating that the thumb print scan had been successful. Immediately after, each SG Watch's face separated down the middle creating two adjacent halves which then expanded and opened up.

"Now remove your gem from the necklace and put em' inside the watch. This is where the gems will be hidden more time" said Tanya. "That's sick!" burst out Rhiarn.

Everyone delicately placed their gems in to the watch, then Tanya smiled and said "That's not even it, there's much more to these watches. Not only can they only be activated by you, they also give you all the system benefits just in case you ever get separated from your suits for some reason... but the best thing of all is the watches also house your suits!"

"No way, that don't even make sense. How can a suit be housed in some little watch?" said Jerome in disagreement.
"I always tell you science and tech is amazing" replied Tanya.
"Yeah' but that's some magic wizardry, juju ting'" responded Jerome.
"Don't I always tell you magic is just science that's hasn't been explained yet" said Tanya
"Anyway, everyone press the switch mode button on the side and hold it down for three seconds" instructed Tanya.

Jay and the teens did as they were told. After three seconds they noticed each SG Suit started to deconstruct then rapidly leave the mannequins and make its way to each individual's watch whilst shrinking along its path.
Everyone was gob smacked as they witnessed the SG Suits compress and amazingly tuck itself into their SG Watches!

Tanya laughed and said "Press and hold the button for three seconds again and let your SG Gems do the rest".
"SG Gems... I like that" mumbled Jay.

Tanya took pleasure from seeing the looks of amazement on everyone's face, she was also extremely proud to see her inventions were working perfectly.

Raheem was the first to press the button again. As

soon as he pressed it the watch face opened and his Purple Star Diamond travelled up his left arm. As the gem travelled around his body, the SG Suit dispatched piece by piece whilst growing and constructing itself on his body following the path of the SG Gem until the SG Gem finally took its place in his necklace's pendant. The rest of the SG Suit then proceeded on its own path to cover the rest of his body and just like that... Raheem was in full SG armour!

The others were mind blown. As soon as they caught themselves they all pressed the button on their SG Watches and suited up too! It was a powerful sight to see, this was the first time the teens ever wore their super hero suits!

"Now you're ready to be super heroes" said Jay. "Just one more thing though... What's super heroes without super hero names?" said Tanya. "I thought about that already. Before you all left Paradise Mountains, did you have any nicknames that people called you?" asked Jay.

Raheem stepped up and said "My mum called me TRUTH".
Rhiarn then said "And she called me SAFA-RHI".
Danny then followed saying "Everyone on my ends' called me PACER".
"Jerome what about you?" asked Jay.
"Everyone just called me Jerome... except my brothers actually, they called me CHUNKSTA".

Then Jay said "That's it then... TRUTH, SAFA-RHI, PACER AND CHUNKSTA and together we'll all be known as SQUAD GIGANTIC!"

Chapter 8 - The Calm Before The Storm!

Months had gone by and as Jay promised Squad Gigantic had been undergoing extremely intensive training! They trained daily in the secret HQ, developing and mastering their powers as well as taking their MMA fighting skills to the highest level.

Due to training and the natural growth of the teens, all their powers developed to new levels! Truth no longer had to wait three seconds to take skills and knowledge. All he had to do was merely touch something and all the knowledge, skills and abilities were directly transferred to him. Progression was easy for him as he could basically pick up anything in just three seconds. Truth instantly became the best fighter in the squad!

Safa-Rhi's powers also reached new heights. Previously she could only control animals and summon their abilities, but now she could also draw directly from Mother Nature herself, allowing her to summon attributes from the weather like lightning, hailstones and thunderstorms!

Pacer developed his fighting skills and his speed continued to break new barriers. His speed coupled with the MMA training made him practically untouchable. Safa-Rhi would often summon the speed of a Cheetah in an attempt to keep up with him, but even that wasn't quick enough! Pacer's speed was like nothing from this World.

Chunksta was a beast, his power grew by the day. In training he had no time for floor work and longs fights, it was all about knock out punches and mega throws. No one could match his power! Every week Jay had to reform those specially made boulders and concrete slabs for Chunksta to use as punch bags.

The Squad Gigantic core values were simple and before every training session they would shout them out:

"A dream's worth nothing if you leave it on a pillow... Believe and Achieve."

"Do right and you'll be done right by... Law of positivity."

"A drop of rain is nothing on its own, but when they form together it's a storm... work together as one."

"Be fearless with righteousness.... Go Get Em'!"

Everything was going smooth for the Gigantic household. The teens continued to live a normal life, studying and doing what regular teenagers do in their everyday lives. They managed to keep their personal identities a secret even though their super hero identities became well-known in London city for stopping numerous crimes and bringing swift justice to criminals such as Da Grabberz. The squad halted everything, from major bank robberies down to assaults on the streets, everyone was speaking about the infamous 'Squad Gigantic'.

It was all getting too easy! But as always when things are running too smooth, it's often a sign that things will change. Jay was so pleased with how things were going that he became complacent. He totally forgot about the biggest threat to Squad Gigantic... Marlo Bang!!!

Jay hadn't heard anything of Bang since he obliterated the Paradise Mountains searching for the SG Gems. Jay always considered the threat of Bang and his army, but he pushed it to the back of his mind as he was convinced he had the teenagers well hidden in plain sight. Bang was a wanted man in London by the police and the streets, so Jay didn't think Bang would dare step foot back here again... but would he?

Meanwhile... somewhere deep in the volcanic Mount Ararat

"Yo Bang... YOO BANG!" shouted Dealer over the noise of drilling.

Bang stopped his attempt at excavating and angrily replied "What is it Dealer? You know I didn't wanna' be interrupted! This better be good you Muppet!" as he took his ear protectors off.

"Relax, trust me you wanna' hear this" replied Dealer with a look of excitement as he went on to say "The Gem Tracker has been going crazy!"

"Rubbish! That hasn't gone off for years mate... since we ripped up those scumbags in Paradise Mountains if I'm not mistaken. You sure it's not broken?" said Bang. "Nar mate, this is the real deal. Thug rock just left the tech guy that Mechanics sent... he's in the plane waiting for a location right now!" replied Dealer.

"Well why we still standing here? Come on let's go!" said Bang.

Bang started moving towards the plane whilst shouting out demands and instructions to his fighting squad, 'Bangz Army'.

Bang and Dealer jumped on the plane.

"Tell me something good Thug Rock, I'm getting fed up of digging in these crappy mountains" said Bang. "I've got some good news and bad news for you boss, well yeah... good and bad but probably good mainly... I think, I'm not really sure!?!" Said a confused Thug Rock. "Well spit it out then!" Blurted out Bang in frustration to Thug

Rock's long winded reply.

"The guy said something about the Gem Tracker has found a high surge of gemstone energy, just like the one that that took us to Paradise Mountains... but the bad news is, it's in your old city... London!" said Thug Rock. "And so what? That's not bad news mate. I've been meaning to pay my hometown a visit, not gonna' let a few pesky warrants and punks stop me! I'm rich now, I'm a King... the King's coming back!" gloated Bang.

Thug rock and Dealer gave each other that look, a look to say finally! Thug Rock and Dealer had been wanting to run through the streets of London for years. They heard all the stories from Bang about his glory days, even though the majority of the tales were exaggerated or even bordering on straight fiction, it still enticed them and planted dreams of causing havoc in London into their brains, they couldn't wait to take over businesses with brut force and control the criminal World on the streets. They both fantasised about London over the last few years, but because of their loyalty to Bang they'd never been to the city as Bang was a wanted man out there.

"But Boss, you've got warrants that will put you in prison for life and what about that Swarvez guy?!?" said a concerned Dealer.

"As I said I'm rich now, I'm a different level to those doughnuts! So stop being a soppy little so and so! You and Thug Rock go ahead of me and find out who I've got to pay to make them nasty little warrants go away! And start sorting out some premises for us to take over. I wanna' play this one carefully, I'll wrap up things here then I'll connect back with you all in a few weeks. Lads, I want to take over that whole city piece by piece and make that our new base for World domination. It's a great day to go home hahahahahahaha" laughed Bang.

"And Dealer, Thug Rock" said Bang.
"Yes Boss" answered his two main goons. "You make sure when I land I'm comfortable, you understand?" said Bang.
They both replied at the same time "The soft way, or the Bang way....?"
"The Bang way of course, by any means necessary!" said Bang.

They both smiled and rubbed their hands together repeating "By any means necessary".

As Thug Rock and Dealer gathered troops from Bangz Army to travel to London with and begin Bang's Reign of terror on the city, Marlo Bang sat there grinning from ear to ear like a kid at Christmas. This is what he had been waiting for, he spent years tracking down the SG Gems. The only gems he didn't possess were the ones in Squad Gigantic's possession. If Bang got a hold of them his quest for World domination would be complete! He would be the unstoppable force of evil.

Chapter 9 - Who's Marlo Bang?

Marlo's Childhood

From an early age Marlo was a problem, but to be honest it wasn't his fault. Growing up in the Bang household the only option in the World was crime. Marlo was the only child of his mother and father, a local gangster couple known in the area as 'The Bangs'. The Bangs were known for anything that involved crime and had a heavy influence in the neighbourhood.

Marlo's parents had their hands in every criminal activity you could think of from importing weapons to bank robbery! In normal abodes most parents would read books to their children at bedtime, but not in this home! From a young age Marlo would be sent to bed watching gangster movies on pirate video tapes to get himself to sleep. This hardly ever worked and most nights Marlo would stay up acting out scenes from his favourite movies like Menace to Society and Scarface, preparing himself for when he got out onto the streets of London. When he would eventually get to sleep he was usually woken by criminals and customers coming in and out of his house or fights that would break out when his parents' deals went sour! Marlo always went to sleep with a weapon under his pillow, he was scared that one day those fights would spill into his room and force him to protect himself.

At face value things looked great for Marlo.

Materially he was spoilt and seemed to have it all. He had all the latest fashions, toys and game consoles. However the horrible truth was that Marlo was neglected and never received any real love from his parents; money and crime always came before him. Marlo's parents would only take him to school if they could be bothered or when they needed to get rid of him for the day, his school attendance was sporadic to say the least. This made things even harder for Marlo as he never really spent enough time in school to build any solid friendships, Marlo always felt alone.

Marlo's only friend was his next door neighbour Jay Gigantic. They were both the same age and were in the same class at school. Jay would often come home from school and ask his mum why Marlo was hardly ever there. She would always reply "When you're older you'll understand, just make sure when he is there you're kind to him" then swiftly change the conversation.

Jay's mum was highly respected in the area, everyone called her 'Mummy G'. She was like the mother of the neighbourhood, she was caring and pleasant but at the same time everyone knew not to mess with her or get on her bad side! Mummy G felt sorry for Marlo and would let him come round to play with Jay when she could sense things were going on in his household. Most mornings Mummy G would knock on the Bang's door offering to take Marlo to school with Jay, but most mornings the door was never answered.

Summer… 22 Years Ago!

It was the six week summer holidays and both Marlo and Jay were only 9 years old. They would play outside together and try to sneak into their local youth club until they were caught and sent home for being too young. Although they both had separate issues at home, they were relatively care free children who ran around playing and doing what typical boys in their area did.

Little did Jay and Marlo know things were about to drastically change and on one tragic day a dreadful event took place that made the boys bond grow stronger.

It was a Thursday morning at approximately 4:30am. Jay was fast asleep, then...
BOOOOOM... "IT'S A ROBBERY NOBODY MOVE!!"
Jay thought he was dreaming and tried to get back to sleep. Then a few moments later Jay was woken again...
BOOM... BANG!!! This time it was by two powerful gunshots!

Jay jumped up scared and ran towards his mum's room, his mum was already in the passage.
"Don't worry son, it's not our house. It's next door" said Mummy G whilst she hugged and comforted Jay who was shaken by the sound of gunshots.
"Come, go back to sleep" gently whispered Mummy G. As they walked back to his room, they heard a frantic knock on the back door!

It was Marlo, he was outside in nothing but a t-shirt and shorts with a pair of unlaced Jordan's on with no socks.

"Help me please, they shot my parents!" begged Marlo as tears streamed down his face.
"Sshhh, quick get in" said Mummy G as she quietly

ushered him in and closed the door whilst cautiously looking around to make sure no one was following him, Mummy G quietly whispered

"This boy better not bring no madness to my door!"

"How many of them was there? Did they see you?" asked Mummy G.

"3 or 4 of them, I don't think they saw me... but I'm not sure" responded Marlo as tears and snot continued to roll down his face.

"Relax, hush everything will be fine" said Mummy G, lying through her teeth trying to assure Marlo that he had nothing to worry about.

Mummy G knew exactly what happened and she knew things would not be alright, but she also knew she had to say and do whatever she could to make Marlo believe everything was fine.

Mummy G called the police. As she peeked through a crack in the front room curtains she saw three people in balaclavas run out of the Bang household with duffle bags filled to the rim with money and weapons. She wasn't surprised at all, it was only a matter of time that things were going to go wrong for the Bangs! Everyone in the area was fed up of them and now there was a new generation of gangsters that had entered the World of crime; a generation that had no respect or fear for the Bang name.

Thirty minutes later they finally saw flashing blue lights and heard sirens. The door knocked and Mummy G sent the boys up to Jay's room.

The police and Mummy G spoke for what felt like forever to the boys, then suddenly they heard Mummy G's gentle footsteps coming up the stairs followed by a much heavier solid pair of feet.

Jay's mum compassionately told Marlo that his parents had been killed and he had to go with the police man. The officer had to literally peel Marlo off of Mummy G as he broke down and cried he locked on to her arm, pulling and ripping her sleeve begging her not to let the police take him away.

Marlo cried and screamed "Don't send me with these Pigs" then repeatedly begged "Can't I just stay here?!?" Until he was finally driven off in the police car.

His parents' murderers were never found and Marlo was placed in care. From this day Marlo's heart turned cold.

Marlo hated it in care, the only thing he liked is that he got to go school more often and see Jay and a few new friends that he had made. Marlo became the ring leader in school, he was loud and always getting into trouble, but because of his situation it was like the teachers would always let him off with minor warnings. Marlo would often run away from his care homes and end up at Jay's house. Mummy G would usually allow him to stay the night, then the authorities would collect him in the morning. This pattern went on for years, he would be in and out of foster homes and constantly have new foster parents. Marlo despised the care system and as soon as he reached the age of sixteen he went to live alone in hostels.

Marlo's Teen Age Years....

Marlo and Jay were both now sixteen and seventeen years old and they were still the best of friends throughout this period and they would often find themselves in tricky situations. Their lives were all about causing trouble, chasing girls or getting into fights and being arrested for petty crimes. Mummy G would be vex anytime she had to collect them from the police station. She started to feel that Marlo was corrupting her precious son and she wasn't going to put up with it any longer.

It was made clear to Jay that his ways would have to change, but unfortunately this didn't work.

Marlo got deeper and deeper into the World of crime. Local gangsters would often give him things to sell and look out for him because they knew his parents. These gangsters showed the same compassion for him that Mummy G used to show, the only problem was their love was shown through crime!

Marlo began to make a serious name for himself on the streets and due to Jay's brains and hustling mentality, he wasn't far behind. Marlo had no remorse for anything he had done! Due to his parents being killed and him having such a rough childhood, he felt the World owed him something and he could never be in the wrong.

Jay's loyalty to Marlo would always be his downfall. Marlo would do some wrong doing that would make Jay have to defend him and get into fights with people Jay never previously had a problem with. Marlo was always wrong and strong and this would constantly put Jay in problems he didn't need to be mixed up in. In the back of Jay's mind he knew that a life of crime was the wrong path to take, but some unexplainable feeling always drew him towards it.

2 Years Later...

At around eighteen/nineteen years old things began to change between Jay and Marlo. Marlo was heavily established in the streets as a real bad man doing robberies and all sorts to make his money. People knew not to mess with him and he was now addressed as 'Bang', continuing his family's criminal legacy.

On the other hand, Jay was finally giving in to his more logical side of thinking and was beginning to go the opposite path from crime. He decided to make a change in his life, the World of crime was no longer for him, something just no longer felt right about it all. He knew he was destined for something greater than this! Mummy G always told him that every ghetto yout' is a star and he's destine to be a King! Jay always shrugged these words off and ignored Mummy G thinking she was just trying to boost his confidence and emotionally trick him into coming off the roads', but now these words began to play on his mind and he was seriously beginning to think the same way! The more thought he gave to his life he realised that the streets were just the perfect place for him to use his business talents to make quick money. As Jay grew older he noticed the harm his actions caused in the community, so he decided it all needed to stop.

Jay figured out a legitimate business plan that if executed correctly could make him millions. It would be life changing; no more crime and street life. He could literally turn his whole world around.
Jay was excited to share his plans with Bang and he even offered him a piece of it. However to Jay's surprise Bang got upset and declined. Bang just loved the street

life too much, it was all he knew and in his mind it was all he was good at. In a sad way, the streets was all Bang thought he had. Even though his persona was big and bad, he was very insecure and his self-value was extremely low.

The news of Jay leaving crime behind was not well received by Bang. He felt betrayed by Jay but rather than let Jay know his feelings, he got bitter and let his mind run. This was never good as he always came to the wrong conclusion.

Bang was upset with Jay and also slightly envious, but what else was new?! As much as Bang would deny it, even as young boys he was jealous of Jay and as they got older it only got worst. Jay was much smarter in the streets than Bang. He also had more morals than Bang and knew how to treat people, so people would always levitate more towards Jay and prefer to do business with him rather than Bang as Bang was so shady. Jay and Bang would often get into arguments as Jay felt Bang was too flashy. Jay was more low key and tried to save his money or invest it elsewhere, whereas Bang was all about showing off and wasting his money on clothes, jewellery and cars, over compensating for his lack of self-esteem. This style of living did nothing good for Bang. It gave him unwanted attention and it often left him broke, forcing him to rob and steal from anyone... even his friends!

Bang believed that since Jay felt he was better than the streets, Jay deserved to lose everything he gained from the streets and he secretly vowed to be the person who took it. Bang went on pretending as if he had no issue with Jay and that he was happy for him, but truthfully it was the total opposite and Bang was conspiring a plan to rob Jay and take all he had.

Winter

Bang played it cool for a long while just plotting and figuring Jay out, trying to see exactly how much cash he had and what would be the best way to set him up. Bang tried extra hard to build Jay's trust and Jay fell for every last bit of it!
Bang finally came up with a plan, in his mind it was perfect! It's was a double bubble, not only would he be able to rob Jay of his money, he would also be able to rob a load of jewellery worth over £200,000!

A guy called Swarvez was bringing in a load of jewellery. Swarvez ran the ends' and he wasn't someone you should mess with! He dressed very well with not one thread out of place. The ladies loved him and the men feared him. Swarvez was heavily connected all over the UK and beyond, only someone as reckless as Bang would try to go against him. However in Bang's mind it was a no brainer, If he executed this plan correctly he could take everything from both parties and he'll be the man.

Summer

By now summertime in London was in full effect. Summer was a special time in the hood as the days were long and fun. Everyone would bring out the Big Whips and Superbikes and both males and females were trying to gain each other's attention in their fresh outfits – this summer was all about Velour tracksuits with Huaraches or designer shorts and designer trainers to match.

Everyone would be out on the block, the olders would be laughing and joking whilst blazing out new music. This year felt like it was the year Grime was invented, the whole of the UK was going crazy for Lethal B's 'Forward Riddim' and every man and his dog would be on the ends' spitting over Wiley's 'Eskimo' beat thinking that their crew was about to be the next big thing in London. The youngers would hang around playing and trying to be a part of the action, hoping one of the generous olders with a little bit of cash would send them to the shop for goodies and tell them to get themselves ice poles and keep the change.

The community was buzzing and the vibes were strong, sure there would be disagreements and arguments but everyone was in such a good mood that they would force those with a problem to squash it and get along.

After a nice day on the ends, Jay went home to kick back and chill with a girl called Tanya who he met beginning of the summer and had been speaking with since. Bang had a crush on the same girl and was secretly upset that she liked Jay instead of him. This fuelled Bang's jealousy to its tipping point! It was the final straw for him. He had a vendetta against Jay and he felt it was now time to execute his plan!

Later that night Bang called Jay to tell him he had the deal of a lifetime!

"Oi Oi Jay, what's going on mate?" Asked Bang. "Nothing G' it's like 2am. You alright, what's good with you?" Replied Jay in a croaky voice whilst he was still half a sleep.

"You know money don't sleep mate, I got a nice cheeky move for us... can make at least 50 large ones each from a little £25k investment... I know you got £25k there bro!" said Bang slyly probing to see what Jay had.
"Slow down bro, slow down" said Jay.
"What's the move? That sounds too good to be true."
Jay was hesitant as Bang always spoke a good one and hardly anything would ever come of it. Bang was forever selling dreams and Jay refused to buy them.

"Trust me this is pukka', it's man like Swarvez... you can call him yourself" replied Bang.
Saying Swarvez name got Jay's attention, Jay respected Swarvez and they'd done loads of business together.
A now wide awake Jay said, "Yeah, man like Swarvez. Them man put me on! From when he's involved I know it's legit... this is what I need to get that last money for my business G".
"That's why I'm giving you a shout mate, I know this is what you need" said the deceitful Bang.
"What is it then?" enquired Jay.
"Them man just done a big move outta' town and hit one of them jewellery vaults. They said they just did it for the cash but on the way out they managed to get the cash and a few trays of top of the range jewellery: Chains, watches, rings, bracelets, you name it!"
"Yeahhh" said Jay becoming even more intrigued.

"Swarvez said there's at least £200k worth of bits there, we can easily flog it on road for a minimum of £100k and he's sayin' we can take it all for 50... tell me you're up for it?" said Bang trying to persuade Jay to put up his cash.

From Bang's calculations, Jay should be sitting on around £20-30k and Bang wanted to take as much of it as possible!
However unknowingly to Bang, Jay grew to be cautious around him. He knew Bang was controlled by greed, so Jay feared that if he showed too much cash and success, one day Bang might go against him! In Jay's heart he never truly felt Bang would betray him, but he also knew it was better to be safe than sorry. So, in actual fact Jay had a lot more than £30k, probably at least double that amount, but he only showed Bang the minimal.

"I'm on it bro, when we doing this?" replied a happy Jay.
"We gotta' move quick before he sells it to them prats' from the other side" said Bang.
"Cool, line it all up for tomorrow" said Jay.
"You got £25k on you like that bro?" said an envious Bang. Bang didn't have this amount of cash so he was filled with even more jealousy when he heard Jay say he had that amount of money around him like it was nothing.

"Come on, you know how I move bro" laughed a cocky Jay.
"Yeah that's how WE move" said Bang lying through his teeth pretending he had the cash too.
"We'll link at the spot tomorrow, I'll bring my half and you bring yours... then we're rich mate" said Bang knowing full well he wasn't bringing any cash.
"Cool bro, ONE" said Jay then he hung up.

Jay was so excited that he couldn't get back to sleep after the phone call 'Finally I can get the last piece of cash needed for my business' he thought. Little did he know it was all a set up.

The Handover!

The next day came and as planned Jay was at the spot. Something felt a bit strange, but he just put it down to paranoia. This was a big life changing deal for Jay, so he thought he was just being unnecessarily nervous.

Bang drove to the spot with his plan in mind. 'It's simple, I'll make Swarvez wait round back and make Jay wait inside. I'll tell Jay to give me the cash so I can do the deal with Swarvez and at the same time I'll tell Swarvez to give me the jewellery so I can show Jay, then I'll slip out the side and escape down the alley with the cash and jewellery'.

To Bang the plan was fool proof! He even planned to lay low for a while after in the countryside with a girl he's been seeing. In Bang's mind it was perfect, it couldn't go wrong. However with Bang being Bang something was bound to go wrong. He never had an eye for detail, every move he made without Jay came with a consequence and collateral damage.

When Bang arrived at the spot, as planned he made Jay wait inside whilst Swarvez was out back, but Bang wasn't aware that Swarvez had two of his goons hiding across the road in a black Focus.

It was all going to plan for Bang until he said to Jay, "I've checked it, it's all good. Pass me your 'arf of the dosh and I'll take it to Swarvez and wrap this all up".

"That's bait, why you gonna do it outside and plus I wanna' see the jewels for myself. You think I'm buying puss in a bag?! Furthermore... why you lot moving funny? Why's he moving like a stranger? It's him who gave me my first O'... he put me on! Tell him to come inside and holla at me, when since we do business like that?" replied Jay.

Bang froze for a second trying to figure out an answer to Jay's request. He couldn't let Jay go out to Swarvez or the whole thing would be messed up.
It was that moment Jay realised something wasn't right. He looked properly at Bang and realised Bang didn't even have a bag with him.

"Hold on, where's your cash?" asked Jay.
For once Bang was quick off the mark and replied "I've given my 'arf to Swarvez already bro, that's what I'm saying it's all cushdy'... just pass your reddies' and I'll deal with it".

Jay was suspicious, he could sense Bang was up to something. Jay decided to play it cool as he didn't know the full extent of the situation, He couldn't tell if it was just Bang or if Swarvez was in on it too.

"Breeze out man, I'm gonna hand him my half directly too... come we go get him" said Jay as he walked ahead towards Swarvez.

Bang didn't know what to do, his plan was all messed

up. As they both walked out to Swarvez a million possibilities and scenarios went through his mind: 'I might not be able to get both the cash and the jewellery, but if I stick up Jay right now I can at least take his money! Or I can go outside and rob the both of them and scarper! But then it'll be two against one... That's it, I can make Swarvez think Jay's setting him up then I can take Jay's cash and hopefully Swarvez will finish off Jay too'.

Jay got out first and Swarvez greeted him with the biggest hug. Swarvez was happy to see Jay, they had a good relationship. Instantly Jay could sense Swarvez was nothing to do with this.

Whilst hugging Swarvez Jay quickly whispered in his ear, "Did Bang give you his cash?"
"Nar not yet youngen" replied Swarvez unknowingly exposing Bang's lie.
"Somethings dodgy with Bang" said Jay quickly warning Swarvez as Bang followed him out.
"Alright say no more" said Swarvez to Jay as he gave his two goons the look. His goons slowly got out the car and creeped over with their hands on their waist as Bang walked out.

Swarvez was an older to Jay and Bang, but Swarvez had a lot of ratings and trust for Jay. So when Jay gave him the warning he didn't think twice on if he should believe him or not, plus Bang had the reputation of a stick up kid. That's why Swarvez sneakingly carried two goons with him in the first place.

Bang frantically stepped outside waving his gun

saying "You mugs' know what it is, I ain't playing no games hand over your bags or get shot".

"You sure you wanna do this?" said Jay whilst Swarvez just laughed.

"What you laughing for Swarvez, I'll do you first!" said Bang, angry that Swarvez wasn't taking his threat seriously.

"You sure bout that?" said Swarvez as he slowly raised his sunglasses to the top of his head saying "My two guys behind you say differently bro".

"Huh, what you talking about?" said Bang as one of Swarvez goons smashed him in his face with a big right hook! Bang's weapon flew out of his hand and he was down.

"Sorry, sorry" pleaded Bang as he was lifted off the ground.

"You really think I would come and link you one up? Furthermore you really think you can rob me and get away with it?" said Swarvez as his two goons held Bang.

They dragged Bang back inside the spot and laid into him.

"You not gonna help me Jay?" begged Bang.

"You just put a gun in my face you fool. Help yourself!" responded a shocked Jay. He couldn't believe Bang would still ask him for help after the stunt he had just pulled.

"You piece of scum. I swear to God, one day I'm gonna' destroy you!" Bang promised Jay.

"Jay I got this bro, if you still want those Jewels... £50k and they're yours bro" said Swarvez.
"I got £25k here now... I can drop you the rest in an hour?" Said Jay

"That's cool bro" replied Swarvez as he instructed one of his goons to give Jay the bag filled with jewellery.

Jay took the jewels and looked over them. Once he was happy with product he shook Swarvez hand, gave him the £25k and made off leaving Bang with Swarvez and his goons. It hurt Jay's heart to have to walk out on Bang in this situation, but he knew Bang brought it on himself.

As Jay got to the top of the road and jumped in his car, he heard three gunshots. In Jays mind he thought that was it, Bangs dead! Jay sat in his car and started to shed a few tears. Even though Bang did what he did they were still once best friends. It destroyed Jay's heart to think Bang was gone.
Jay quickly drove away whilst wiping tears, he didn't want to be around when the police came.

A few hours went past and Swarvez called Jay from a private number. Swarvez arranged to meet Jay on the outskirts of the city to collect the remaining £25k he had for him.
They linked up at a service station on the M4 motorway.

"Your homie Bang is lucky bro" said Swarvez with the most serious look on his face.
"That ain't my homie no more... but what d'you mean?" asked Jay.

"As I said, he's a lucky yout'! He got away" replied Swarvez.

"But I heard shots" said Jay.

"Yeah you did, one from him... about two from us G" said Swarvez.

Jay said "For real, you didn't merk' him?".

It was bittersweet for Jay. One half of Jay was happy that Bang wasn't actually dead, but the other half of him knew that one day Bang would come back and be a problem.

"Nar as you left he managed to grab his stick off the floor and shoot one of my homies in his arm, then he ran off! We bust' two after him, but they missed and it was too bait to chase him on the main road... he got away. When I see him though he's finished. I put the word out and the whole ends is looking for him now... we' soon catch him!" promised Swarvez.

Jay gave Swarvez his cash and went on his way.

As planned, Jay took the jewellery and sold it then invested the cash into his business. The business was property development. Jay put deposits down on properties, renovated them and then he sold them on for profit. This gave Jay and Mummy G a whole new lifestyle, one far away from the streets. Unfortunately whilst this was happening in Jay's life, Bangs life continued to spiral in the total opposite direction.

Chapter 10 - Bang's Come Up

Bang's Adulthood!

Life started to go extremely wrong for Bang since his attempt to rob Jay and Swarvez. Bang no longer had Jay by his side to clean up his mess and to make things worse the whole of his neighbourhood was now against him. People who didn't even know Bang wanted his blood just to prove their loyalty to Swarvez.

For at least five to six years Bang ran around London's streets robbing everyone he could in order to survive. Things got so bad that he had to start hanging out with the other side... well, until he robbed all of them too. Eventually the World got smaller and smaller for Bang until he had nowhere to run. All the money from his robberies had run out and so had his luck. Bang was flat on his face not knowing what to do next. He had no money or food and wasn't sure how he was going to survive, he had officially hit rock bottom. He was so low that he stole a cup of coins from a homeless man that was sleeping on the pavement. Bang counted the coins, it was exactly £4.53! With no remorse whatsoever Bang got himself 2 pieces of chicken and chips then walked into a newsagents to buy a pineapple soda. Bang had £2 remaining and saw the National Lottery had a triple rollover jackpot of £80million! So just for the fun of it, Bang decided to buy a Lottery Ticket.

A few days went by and Bang was laying low at his girlfriend's house. His girlfriend was a lady called Elisha, Elisha Bossiá. She was a beautiful tanned lady with the perfect body shape. She was into high end fashion and came from a rich family. Elisha was a girl Bang knew from out of town. He met her on a trip he took with Jay. Bang noticed her as they sat and ate in a restaurant. Bang fell for her right there and then. He spoke with her and ran enough game to get her phone number. They spoke for a while and grew closer. Bang would stay with her at hotels any time he had to travel to the area and conduct illegal business.

Elisha was from a really good family, but she was intrigued by Bang and the street life. Her family didn't approve of her seeing Bang once they learnt of his background and eventually they made her make a choice between them and him. This backfired on her family as Elisha chose Bang. Since that day they'd lived together in a council flat out in the sticks. The only other person that knew about Elisha was Jay, but he never knew where her new address was. Bang felt safe out in the sticks, it was a new start in a place where nobody knew him.

It was a cold Saturday evening. Bang sat on the sofa with Elisha eating pie and mash whilst watching TV. The Lottery came on the screen. Remembering he had a ticket, he jumped up and got it out of his jacket pocket in the passage. Bang came back in the room and told Elisha that he actually played the Lottery this week. They laughed and joked about what they would do if they won the jackpot. Elisha said she would buy a mansion with walk in wardrobes and fill it with designer clothes, shoes, bags and expensive jewellery. Bang didn't tell Elisha what he would do, all he did was laugh and say, "No one from my neck of the manor ever wins the Lottery" then he tucked into his steak and kidney pie.

Elisha sighed at his negativity and responded saying "You not in that neck of the manor no more, you're a country boy now luv".

As they sat eating dinner, the TV presenter called out the lottery numbers.
Bang almost choked on the pastry.

"I won... Oi I WON!" shouted Bang.
"Won what babes" said Elisha.
"The Lottery... 80 bloody million!!" blurted out Bang as he jumped around the room going crazy.
They doubled checked the numbers and it was true...
Bang won the Lottery.
The TV presenter went on to say "Early indications show that there is only one lucky jackpot winner this week".
Not only did Bang win, he was the only person to hit the jackpot that week! The whole £80 million was his.

Bang and Elisha finally calmed down from all the excitement, then Elisha asked "Seriously, what do want to do with the money?"
Bang jokingly replied "First thing I should do is chuck that tramp I robbed a tenner hahahaha"
"You're a wrongen' babes, seriously tho... what you gonna' do with it?" Asked Elisha
"You'll probably laugh at me and tell me I'm a nutta" said Bang as he looked down at the ground
"I already think you're a mad man so you might as well

try me babes" joked Elisha.

"When I was younger Mummy G used to tell me and Jay stories bout' a place called Paradise Mountains, she said it's the centre of the Earth or something" explained Bang.

"Arrrr, you wanna go there on a romantic holiday?" asked Elisha. "Nar" laughed Bang.

"It's more complicated than that anyway, you can't just go there... it's protected. Jay's mum used to talk about some special gemstones and some chosen ones" said Bang.

"Well you can buy £80 million worth of them now luv" gloated Elisha.

"Just be quiet and listen. You can't buy these gems they're priceless! Anyway as I was saying, these jewels and other ones around the World possess powers. Powers that can control the whole World! If I can get hold of these gems I can be the most powerful person to exist!" The gems are all over the World in different mountains, well all apart from the Chosen One's gems... they're in Paradise Mountains! I never had the money to go and look for them before" said Bang.

"So what are you saying babes?" asked Elisha. "I'm saying as soon as this money comes through, I'm going to travel the World and collect these gemstones one by one and then take over the World... that simple!" declared Bang.

"You're right I do think that you're crazy" said Elisha. "But that's why I love you, let's do it together... Every King needs his Queen" said Elisha as she kissed Bang on his forehead.

As soon as the money came through Bang set off around the World searching for the gemstones. Bang also opened up multiple businesses so his cash would grow and never run out. He realised this journey would be dangerous in many ways, so he continued to train in MMA and he also built a protection team that he named 'Bangz Army'. Bangz Army was a team of loyal no nonsense fighters and soldiers who lived for Bang and his command. They literally followed Bang to the end of the World and back. This made Bang a force to be reckoned with!

Bang travelled to loads of mountains around the World digging and ripping into the mountain's rocks until he found whichever gemstone he was looking for; sometimes he was successful sometimes he wasn't. A lot of times he found much more than he bargained for, acquiring Diamonds and Rubies that had no special powers but were worth millions. He would sell them and add even more cash to his bankroll. However, even better than Diamonds and riches along his journey he found two unbelievable gifts. Two people who would join his army and add a strength that no mortal man could fight against... Bang named them Thug Rock and Dealer!

Thug Rock and Dealer were both unexpectedly found in different mountains on different explorations. Both Thug Rock and Dealer had super powers which they ascertained whilst stranded in the mountains. Bang was amazed by their abilities and saved them both from their situations promising them a stake in running the World if they help him complete his mission by locating and retrieving all the gemstones from Paradise Mountains and the rest of World.

Dealer

Dealer was found in the Himalaya's. He was the only child of a billionaire couple who ran the World's biggest import and export company. His father was a fully qualified pilot and would often take his family on holidays in their private jet. At the age of twelve years old the father flew Dealer and his mum out to China on his private jet. Before departing to go China, Dealer's father was warned that the weather conditions were not safe to fly in, however his father was a proud and arrogant man so he decided to ignore the warnings and flew his family anyway. The flight was rocky to say the least! The plane was constantly being thrown from side to side by turbulence. Dealer was scared, so his mum played him at Black Jack to distract him from the journey, but the treacherous weather just got worse.

About ten minutes into playing cards tragedy struck! Dealer's father tried to fly lower in the hope of avoiding the turbulence and in doing so he lost control of the plane and crashed directly into Mount Everest. Dealer's parents were burnt to ashes when the plane's engines exploded, but luckily before the plane burst into a mega fireball, the impact from the force of the crash threw Dealer out of the plane.

Dealer was knocked unconscious when he collided with the mountain's rocks. When he eventually woke up he found nothing but a few playing cards that he was somehow gripping tightly in his right hand. His other arm was impaled in a cluster of large White Diamonds. At this time Dealer didn't realised these White Diamonds were special gemstones that possessed powers. The majestic gemstones amalgamated with Dealer and oozed its powers into his bloodstream via his left arm, giving Dealer abilities he could only dream of.

As Dealer tried to release himself from the Diamond cluster, he noticed a large animal-like creature coming towards him. He was scared witless! He tried to scream for help, but it was useless as nobody was there! The creature kept coming closer and closer. As the creature got nearer, Dealer's fear grew stronger... It was a Yeti!

A vicious looking Gorilla-like animal at least 8ft tall with white fur and big sharp teeth with saliva dripping off its canines. Dealer froze with fear, knowing this creature could eat him whole!

As the Yeti reached a few feet from him, Dealer closed his eyes and gripped the one card he still had in his hands, it was a King of Hearts. The card magically developed a full Diamond casing then went back to normal in what couldn't have been any longer than two seconds! As this happened Dealer saw the same Diamond casing form in the Yeti's eyes. Rather than attack, the Yeti came to a halt and then slowly walked over to Dealer and yanked his arm out of the Diamond cluster then carried him to safety. Dealer realised that somehow he had managed to hypnotize or take control of the Yeti and make it protect him. Since that day Dealer lived in a cave deep within Mount Everest with the Yeti... until Bang found him.

Amazingly the Yeti protected him from all the threats of the mountain, loving Dealer as if he was his own pup.

As Dealer grew older he learnt how to take control of his powers. He kept the three remaining playing cards he had left and protected them with all his strength, as he felt they had given him the ability to control minds. The powers bestowed on to Dealer from the Diamond cluster combined with the cards due to him having a grip on them whilst the powers entered his body. Touching each playing card allowed different things to happen:

The King of Hearts - takes control of minds, blinding the victim with love for Dealer and making the victim do anything he wants them to do.

The Jack of Spades - has the power to control people and make them go to war for him.

The Ace of Diamonds - this card has the power to make the victim steal anything that's equates to currency for Dealer.

The Yeti built Dealer's strength by wrestling with him in the same manner a Silverback Gorilla would wrestle with its pups. It was an amazing sight to see, daily they would have playful battles on mountain tops. The Yeti was always delicate enough to never cause Dealer any real harm. Dealer's powers ensured that the beast was always led by an unmeasurable amount of love for him.

In the Himalayas Dealer's abilities came in handy, especially the powers he acquired from the Ace of Diamonds. In mainland society currency would be things like money and Diamonds, however in the Himalayas the currency is food and water! With the Yeti being firmly controlled by Dealer's spell, it hunted food and gathered water for him each and every day. This was the only reason Dealer survived on the mountains.

When Bang arrived at Mount Everest he saw Dealer wrestling with the Yeti. Unaware of Dealer and the Yeti's relationship, Bang fired his rifle and shot the Yeti in its back firmly believing he was saving Dealer from a deadly attack. However his erratic actions proved to be the very thing that put Dealer in harms way! The shot's connection was so powerful that it instantly took the Yeti out of Dealer's spell. The Yeti reformed back to its natural ways of a predator and attacked Dealer and a number of Bangz Army before escaping into the mountains.

Dealer realised without the Yeti's protection there would be no way he could survive in the Himalayas. He informed Bang of his special powers in the hope of proving his worth to him. A new intelligent Bang saw Dealer's worth straight away but before accepting him into the army he warned Dealer that if he ever used his powers on him he will be killed. Dealer accepted the terms and to prove his loyalty to Bang, he took Bang to the Diamond cluster. Bang took the main gems out of the cluster, packed it up and went on his way.

Thug Rock

Thug Rock's story was a bit different. He didn't come from a rich family, as a matter fact he didn't have a family at all. Thug Rock was abandoned at the tender age of three years old; he couldn't even remember his name. Thug Rock was the name given to him once Bang found him. He came from a small village in Tanzania, Africa. His first memory was a horrible heart wrenching one of his village being ambushed! All he recalls is gunshots flying around and his home being burnt down with men, women and children being slaughtered!

Whilst Thug Rock's father fought to defend the village, he commanded Thug Rock's mother to abscond with Thug Rock, firmly instructing her to go to the river and escape on his fishing boat.
Thug Rock's mother grabbed him and made a run for it. She covered him in an ancient traditional cloth, hoping it would blind his vision from all the terror and destruction surrounding them. As instructed, she headed towards the river that ran through a nearby village where the father's fishing boat was anchored, but as she got to the river she noticed the aggressors were close!

Thug Rock's mother had to make the hardest decision of her life! She had to give herself up to save her precious son or they may both have been captured and killed! She kissed Thug Rock on his forehead and told him to never forget her and his father, then she placed him on the boat, lifted the grapnel anchor and pushed him to float downstream.
After making such a devastating decision, she quickly

ran back to the aggressors and handed her self over so they wouldn't notice Thug Rock floating away. His mother was shown no mercy and as Thug Rock floated away he heard a bone chilling scream from his mother as she was executed.

Thug Rock washed up near the Kilimanjaro Mountains where he was miraculously taken in by a family of Blue Monkeys. As Thug Rock grew older he had to hunt to eat. He would make weapons out of wood and rock to kill wild animals. Every day he drank from a majestically colourful spring that sprung out in the section of the mountain he made his home. Water would emerge out a cluster of precious stones, but Thug Rock never realised the clusters value as the water was the only thing that was important to him.

Thug Rock grew extremely strong from hunting and battling with large Mousses and other mountain animals. As he grew older he realised his forearms were changing, they were solidifying and turning to rock. Thug Rock was unaware that the spring he drank from daily was contaminated by special gemstones with powers and abilities. The spring gave Thug Rock powers. His hands turned to rock and he soon learnt he had the ability to spray rocks out from his fist.

At first Thug Rock was scared of these abilities and he would try his hardest to get rid of it, but all his efforts were pointless as the more he tried to lose them the more they grew stronger. Thug Rock eventually accepted his powers and even began to use them to his benefit, whilst hunting he would shoot rocks from his fists at prey to knock them unconscious before completing his hunt.

When Bang and his army arrived on Mount Kilimanjaro, Thug Rock immediately engaged them in battle and took out at least thirty soldiers! Thug Rock was an unstoppable force. Eventually Bang and Dealer tamed him using a Tranquilliser Gun. Bang once again saw the benefits of adding this super human to his army. Bang named him 'Thug Rock' and immediately showed him a different way of living alongside promising him revenge for his village if he joined Bangz Army.

Bang spent the next few days in Mount Kilimanjaro showing Thug Rock a different side to life, introducing him to foods and drink and showing him technology he had never seen before. Thug Rock began to enjoy the life Bang was showing him and this led him to agree to join Bangz Army.

Thug Rock eventually took Bang to the colourful spring which he drank from ever since he had been on the mountains. He told Bang to look beyond the water springing out. Bang listened and noticed a cluster of gems. Without an ounce of hesitation Bang pushed his hand through the transparent water and grabbed the gems out the cluster right there and then. Bang had found what he came for and didn't want to spend anymore time on Mount Kilimanjaro, he placed his arms on Thug Rock's shoulder and said, "Tonight's the night I honour my word mate". It was time to get Thug Rock's revenge!

Bang, Dealer, Thug Rock and Bangz Army travelled across a number of villages in Tanzania in the hope that Thug Rock's memory would eventually identify the village he was born in. The journey took longer than they expected. Each night they pitched their tents and gathered fire wood hoping they were one step closer to their target. This went on for days and everyone but Thug Rock was close to giving up. Then finally whilst on an early morning trek, Thug Rock found a village that gave him a feeling so familiar that it sent chills down his spine. As he scoped out the village, he arrived at an area near the lake where he last remembered seeing his mother. As he stood there, in his mind he could hear the scream she bellowed out as she died!

It was definitely his village, but unfortunately it had been taken over by a corporate company from the USA. Many years had gone by since they exterminated all the village's original residents to take over the goldmines and profit from the precious commodity. To Thug Rock's disgust these evil cowards were now fully established in this area! There was no trace of his heritage and no sense of remorse from the trespassers who killed his people to steal his families land.

Bang looked into Thug Rock's eyes and instantly saw the pain in his heart. Bang immediately empathised and related to Thug Rock's sorrow as a fellow orphan who saw his parents be murdered. To honour Thug Rock's family, Bang decided to allow him to lead Bangz Army in this battle. Thug Rock accepted the opportunity with pride then went forward and remorselessly destroyed everything and everyone in the honour of his family and ancestors. Bangz Army reigned terror on all of these trespassers with Thug Rock taking extreme pleasure in getting his revenge! However the victory was bitter sweet for Thug Rock as there was even less of his former village left once the ambush was over.

Realising the Village was uninhabitable, Thug Rock pledged his allegiance to Bang. Bang was so impressed by Thug Rock's strength and ruthlessness that he immediately gave him the role of being his right hand man alongside Dealer.

Chapter 11 - Here Comes The Bang!

A few months went pass and it was time for Bang's homecoming! Thug Rock and Dealer had done exactly what they planned to do; they locked down the city and rapidly made Bangz Army the most feared gang in the whole of London.

Thug Rock gathered the most active and influential members of Da Grabberz and called a meeting. Swarvez was getting on in age but he was still the boss of the gang he created. Thug Rock told Swarvez that he and all the other Grabberz had a simple choice... join Bangz Army or be destroyed! As expected, Swarvez disagreed and decided to fight back, this didn't go well for him at all! Bang heard of Swarvez disobedience and told Thug Rock to ruthlessly dispose of him in front of all the Grabberz to not only prove a point, but to also finally get revenge for what took place way back in the day.

Thug Rock did as he was ordered and put Swarvez through a horrible ordeal in front of his gang, which eventually led to the death of Swarvez. From this day all the Grabberz fell in line with Bang's regime and that was the end of "Da Grabberz" as we knew it. They all joined Bangz Army and now took lead from Dealer and Thug Rock. Even though this was effectively the end of Da Grabberz, it took the ex-Grabberz to a new level! Having access to Bang's resources allowed them to move at a higher level of criminal intelligence and activity.

Da Grabberz joining Bangz Army was perfect for

Bang. Him being a wanted man on the streets was one of the main reasons he went into exile in the first place. As well as being a takeover, this was a smart tactical move because now everyone who would've previously been hunting him was now under his command. The Bang family name was truly back in power! The only thing left to clean up was Bang's legal matters.

Thug Rock and Dealer proceeded in clearing Bang's name on a legal level by paying off corrupt police and dodgy politicians. If the police and politicians didn't agree to the terms set, Thug Rock would use brut force and violence to change their mind.

Bang was adamant that Thug Rock and Dealer must be discreet in the takeover, keeping all criminal activity on a need to know basis.
Bang set clear orders to come across as a respectable business firm to the public eye. Dealer's brain power allowed them to execute this role perfectly, they acquired a number of high end properties and opened multiple businesses all around the city as fronts:

Ace Of Clubs - Dealer's night club that he always dreamed of owning.

Bossiá Jewels - A jewellery shop in Elisha's name where Bang could sell the powerless gems and precious metals he's found on his quest.

Marlo's Shipping Co. – An import, export and haulage company that Bang could use to get his illegal contraband sent around the World without any trace.

Rock Hard Security - Thug Rock's security company

filled with members of Bangz Army. Thug Rock used his firm to strong arm his way into companies via security and then extorted the businesses in return for his protection... from him!

MB Rentals - Bang's car rental company where him and his army could switch transport daily without any suspicion or hassle from the police.

Everything was going to plan for Thug Rock and Dealer, everything except... Squad Gigantic!

As soon as Thug Rock and Dealer got into town, Jay knew something was suspicious. The random death of Swarvez, Da Grabberz going silent and then Bangz Army popping up and creating a crazy crime spree in a manner that was more sophisticated than any crimes this city had ever seen before. Jay immediately set Squad Gigantic on to Bangz Army whilst he personally investigated who was behind them.

Squad Gigantic were on the streets ripping through Bangz Army bringing major robberies and heists to a halt, saving London city from catastrophic events. Meanwhile Jay couldn't seem to get any real information on Bangz Army. Everyone's mouth was sealed! Due to the name 'Bangz Army' he was certain that Marlo Bang was behind it all, but when he spoke with his sources the names he frequently heard were Thug Rock and Dealer.
Jay knew these names from somewhere but for the life of him, he couldn't remember where from.
This wrecked Jay's brain for days and to make things worse he couldn't even put a face to these names as

Thug Rock and Dealer were smart enough to stay in backgrounds with fake identities posing as reputable business men who didn't want any attention that comes along with their faces being known.

Dealer reported back to Bang informing him of their successes and problems.
Bang was catching up with his daily dose of his favourite Snapchat star -Stevo the madman, as he rolled around in laughter he was interrupted by a phone call from Dealer

"Dealer, how's it going in London mate?" asked Bang.
"Boss, everything's sweet... well almost everything. But we're nearly ready for you" replied Dealer.
"What d'you mean almost? What's going on!?" shouted Bang.
"Well, all the businesses are in place and all the gangs are in order... from that aspect we're cool" said Dealer.

"So what's your problem?" said Bang, his smile slowly left his face as he became more and more agitated by Dealer's stalling.
Dealer hesitantly replied, "It's every time we hit the streets, there's some kinda' gang of do gooder' teens called Squad Gigantic running around and messing up every move our army makes".

Bang screamed down the phone, "You mean to tell me our army of fighters and killers are getting put to shame by a bunch of kids?! You better get this sorted! A big portion of our incomes' from the street stuff! I can't believe you got some little brats messing it up" said Bang.

"Boss you don't understand, these kids are something else. From the reports I'm getting it's like they got some sort of powers, it's like they're similar to me and Thug Rock" said Dealer trying to bring some pride back to the situation.

"I'm sure me and Thug could go out and deal with them... but that means us blowing our cover and putting the whole project at risk" said Dealer.
"Just relax, I'm flying over tonight. I'll sort this mess out when I reach" said a much calmer Bang as he hanged up and went back to watching the STMM Snapchat stories.

Initially Bang was furious to hear about Squad Gigantic and in his heart he knew straight away that only one man could be behind them, Jay Gigantic! Who else would call their squad 'Gigantic'?
However, at the same time Bang was actually quite happy. These teens with super powers could be exactly what he's looking for... they must hold the gems! Also with Jay leading them he could kill two birds with one stone and destroy his long-time nemesis. That very same night Bang flew in to London with Elisha and they spent their first night in their new mansion on the outskirts of town.

Chapter 12 - Work Together As One

Bang was finally ready to show his face and make his mark on London. He wanted to make a major statement, showing all the people that thought he was down and out that Bang's back with a bang!

However Bang was well aware that he had to play it smart. He finally understood that the Tortoise always beats the Hare.

So Bang played it cool. He came back and portrayed himself as a reformed man. Bang embedded himself as a pillar of the community and a very high profile business man. Jay saw Bang in London newspapers and heard him on local radio stations claiming he's a model citizen, Jay wasn't believing any of it.

Jay knew Bang had an ulterior motive and in his mind, Jay knew exactly what that motive was. As far as Jay was concerned, Bang was still on his quest for the gems and somehow he found out the gems were here in London. Everything began to make sense in Jay's mind. He put two and two together and got four, he was happy to finally make sense of everything but unfortunately this clarity also confirmed his fears.

'This means my youts' are at risk. If Bang knows that they got the SG Gems, he's gonna' come at them with everytin' he's got!' thought Jay. Jay knew he had to defeat Bang and the only way to do this was to get the teens up to a level they've never had to perform at before.

As Jay sat down to think things through, he had a major realisation. 'Thug Rock and Dealer, that's who they are... Bang's henchmen!' realised Jay, finally remembering exactly where he heard their names before.

"Them man were part of the attack on Paradise Mountains" whispered Jay as he visualised the exact moment when he saw them and heard Bang say their names.

"Thug Rock was the brudda' who had the hands made of rocks... the one that smashed the waterfall and Dealer's the one who Bang sent to gather gems" mumbled Jay to himself.

"MADDD TINGGG!" shouted Jay.
Jay was getting hyped up now, he was angry and ready for war. No way was he allowing anyone to cause harm to his children. Jay felt the fight running through his veins and decided it was time to get teens ready for a fight too.

Jay explained the situation to the team and then Squad Gigantic went into extreme intense training. Everyone understood this would be the biggest challenge they'd faced so far, well everyone except Pacer! Pacer's arrogance didn't allow him to see the seriousness of the situation, his speed made him feel he was invincible.

This was an ongoing problem with Pacer, he would often arrive late to training and was more interested in partying, looking good to his friends and going on dates with girls rather than developing his skills and this made

Truth angry!

The next day training commenced at the usual time of 6am in Squad Gigantic's secret HQ.
Everyone was there on time except Pacer who was still in bed sleeping after a night out with his friends.
Tempers were boiling and the team were getting frustrated.
Jay came in and asked everyone "Where's Pacer?!"
Everyone looked around with a look of disappointment, but no one wanted to snitch on him.
"Boyyyyy... I don't know and to be real, I don't even care, he's jarrin' me man" said Chunksta.
"It's true, he's moving like a little eediot'!" added Safa-Rhi.

"STOP THAT!" shouted Jay putting an immediate end to the slander.
"What's value three?" asked Jay, looking firmly at the squad members that were present.
"A drop of rain is nothing on its own, but when they form together... it's a storm" said Squad Gigantic in perfect synchronisation.

"Exactly we work together as one" said Jay. "This is isn't just stopping little bank robberies and crimes in the area no more, this is a major force of evil! You saw what they done to Paradise Mountains... YOUR HOME! They're not a joke. The only way we're gonna' defeat them is by working together and performing at our best abilities. I don't wanna' hear anyone putting anyone down, even if they are messing up... d'you understand?!" Said Jay.

"Yes Jay" replied Safa-Rhi, Truth and Chunksta.
"Let me go get him" said Truth.

Truth's anger continued to grow as he went upstairs to get Pacer. Truth ran into his room and punched him straight in his stomach.
"Get up! Why you still in bed?" shouted Truth.
"Arghh, allow me man... what time is it?" asked Pacer.
"It's training time you eediot' and you're in bed like some wasteman!" replied Truth.
"Rah' sorry I'm coming now bro" said Pacer as he got out of bed and held his stomach to ease the pain.

"Sorry ain't good enough bro, we're in a madness right now! We're at war with some real bad man. These people destroyed our home fam', wiped out our families... and you're here messing around! You're more interested in raving and gyal'. Fix up bro, seriously or you're gonna' get us all bodied!" explained Truth trying his best to reach out to his younger brother.

"I'm coming now, I'll be down before you G" said Pacer. As Truth walked down to training, Pacer used his speed and was literally fully dressed and in HQ within seconds!

"Nice of you to join us mate" said Jay sarcastically to Pacer.

As Pacer apologised, Safa-Rhi shouted out "Urrgggghhh you tramp!" "What?" said Pacer.
"You and your stinkin' breath! You mean to tell me it takes you a matter of seconds to do anything and you couldn't quickly brush your nasty teeth" said Safa-Rhi in

disgust.

Chunksta rolled on the floor laughing and an embarrassed Pacer told his sister "shut up" whilst discreetly putting his hand over his mouth to check his breath.

"Calm down and focus" said Jay.

"Pacer go brush your teeth and when you come back you're doing 200 laps in the Velocitizer... 100 for your lateness and another 100 laps just for your nastiness. I don't know how you get so much girls with your dirty ways" rambled on Jay.

The squad continued to train and gain from their sessions. Pacer's attitude eventually improved and he understood the importance of the possible battle that was ahead.
The training took Squad Gigantic to another level! Everyone's abilities enhanced even further.
Truth's mind power had developed to such a high level that he was able to move items a few inches with just his brain power alone, however this power had not been fully mastered yet and would leave him weak if used to frequently.

Safa-Rhi's abilities enhanced to a new level that allowed her to also control and summon natural disasters like earthquakes, tornados, hurricanes and even volcanos. She also mastered the art of the eagle and was now able to confidently fly.

Pacer's speed developed to such a high velocity that he could give the illusion of teleportation within a one mile radius. He could literally run on air, he had finally advanced to 'Speed King' status. Tanya also added an amazing upgrade to his suit, a pair of direct energy boosters that shoots out highly focused energy laser blasts which are powered by the force of his speed coupled with the power within his Golden Beryl.

Now puberty had kicked in, Chunksta's power got to an immeasurable state. Every week Tanya would upgrade the Mega D, but Chunksta's powers will still register off the scale. Chunksta could go through anything, not even a tank could stop him.

Weirdly Jay even noticed a change in himself, this was rather strange because as far as he knew he never had any abilities. However Jay felt himself getting stronger and noticed slight changes to his body. He thought nothing of it and put his development down to him delivering the intense training to the squad.

Chapter 13 - Patience Is A Virtue

Bang's guys had no chance. The mix of intense training coupled with the new gadgets from Tanya allowed Squad Gigantic to reign supreme on Bangz Army each and every time they committed a crime. Bangz Army couldn't get away with anything in London.

A frustrated Bang had to change his strategy and create a new approach, Squad Gigantic managed to force him into a corner he didn't expect to find himself in. No longer could Bang play the patient game, his army wasn't bringing in any cash from the streets he had to solely rely on his legal businesses for cash, which was no good as they were mainly fronts and cover ups to wash his illegal money. Bossiá Jewels was the only business that was profitable for him.

The rest of the underworld was losing faith in Bang as his promise to take care of Squad Gigantic looked like nothing but hot air. Squad Gigantic had the whole underworld shaken up, everyone was scared to make a move in London... it was officially Squad Gigantic's city.

Bang decided he couldn't wait any longer, it was time to make his move. He had no option but to bring Thug Rock and Dealer out of the background and put them on to the battlefield! Bang began strategizing, over the years he became much more cunning and gained a lot of intelligence. The old Bang would've gone rushing in with all guns blazing and eventually mess things up, but not anymore. Bang decided to set traps to catch Squad

Gigantic, he planned a quick string of events: a robbery and a kidnap - with the aim of each event having a particular desired outcome.

The first robbery took place at the London City Museum, Bang sent in a team to steal a precious Asante Gold Crown. He set strict instructions for his army not to engage in battle as Bangz Army numbers were getting uncomfortably low due to the clean-up Squad Gigantic had been performing. The aim of the robbery was simply for Bang to see Squad Gigantic for himself and finally unmask these infamous teens.

As planned, Bangz Army ran in at midnight and purposely set off the alarm which automatically sent an alert to London City Police (LCP), which was intercepted by Tanya's SG System. Tanya was woke by the signal and dispatched the teens to the London City Museum.

Bang had his tech guy 'Mechanics' remotely hack into the museum's CCTV and send a feed to his phone so he could watch it all go down play for play. Bangz Army lured the teens inside the museum and hid where the teens couldn't see them. In hot pursuit of Bangz Army, Squad Gigantic ran right into Bang's trap – a bright room with perfect lighting that allowed Bang to get a clear shot of each teens face. As the teens entered the room, Bangz Army members threw smoke bombs to obscure the their view and in the chaos they ripped the mask of each teens face then immediately dispersed from the museum back to their hide out.

The squad stood in the cloud of smoke confused as to what was happening. Their faces were exposed for now longer than five seconds... but that was five seconds too long! Pacer, Truth, Chunksta and Safa-rhi quickly covered their faces and got in position to fight! Only to find out they were in an empty room with the Gold Crown still in its cabinet as the smoke cleared.

Truth telepathically asked Safa-Rhi "What's going on?" "I'm not sure but somethings dodgy, they didn't even take the Crown ting'" replied Safa-Rhi straight back in his mind.

Then Truth told everyone "Let's give this building a once over and get out of here. Let the jakes deal with this one".

The teens checked over the museum and discovered nothing seemed to be taken. Then they reported back to Tanya and Jay through their comms system.

"Maybe the SG System has a glitch" said Safa-Rhi to Tanya via his comms.
"No, the alarm was definitely set off and the room was full of smoke" replied Tanya.
"That's true, maybe it was just some youts' messing around" said Safa-Rhi.
"I don't know what it was, but I do know something's dodgy. I don't like it, get out of there and get back to base" instructed Jay.

The teens exited the museum and made their way back home.

Things ran perfectly for Bang. Mechanics sent him a few face shots that he managed to capture from the footage of the feed, Bang was chuffed he reclined his chair back and rapped along to Linguo by Giggs as he was being chauffeured to his HQ by Thug Rock. Bang stopped rapping for a second to look at the CCTV images and at this point he realised exactly who the teens were.

"Oi turn that down mate" said Bang.
As Thug Rock reluctantly muted his favourite rappers track Bang grinned like a Cheshire Cat and asked him "You know who they are don't ya?"
"Nar, who are they?" said Thug Rock.
"You can't tell? Guess" replied Bang.
"I ain't got a clue boss, you might as well tell me or we gonna' be here all day" laughed Thug Rock.
"It's those kids" said Bang.
"What kids?" said Thug Rock with a look of bemusement.
"Those kids from Paradise Mountains you dummy. Remember the kids Jay got away with on his plane. It all makes sense now. They protected them because they have powers!" said Bang.
"Look at this pic. This boy has gotta' be the one that one of the killer Panthers attacked. Look he's still got the scar on his face to prove it" said Bang whilst showing Thug Rock an image and pointing at Truth.
"Oh yeah and that's the other two kids that ran ahead. But who's that little hench one?" said Thug Rock. "That must but the young one who had the big man chest?" said Bang as they both busted out laughing. "Yeah I remember him now, I swear down I killed his father… the brudda' looked just like him but taller… the man could fight still, But I whacked him up" said Thug rock.

As Bang laughed, Thug Rock looked at him and asked

"Quick question boss, why didn't we just grab them there and then in the museum?"

"Over the years I've learnt that patience is a virtue mate. I wanna' know exactly who they are and what we're dealing with. Just be easy, when the times right we'll grab em' all" said Bang as he turned back up the music and continued to sing "Shout out to my bruddas' on the wing tho" whilst doing the silliest dance as they approached their HQ.

Now Bang had confirmed his suspicions on who Squad Gigantic were, he decided to put the second part of his plan in motion.

Bang planned to kidnap the Mayor's daughter and hold her hostage on the roof top of Marlo's Shipping Co. He didn't plan to hurt her but he wanted to send a firm message to the Mayor that Bang was still in charge of London whilst cleverly luring out Squad Gigantic again.

Marlo's Shipping Co. was the perfect location to discreetly hold a hostage as it was located in an area that was basically derelict and abandoned. Apart from Marlo's Shipping Co. there were only one or two other businesses in this area. Bang's building sat over the docks and was situated right on the edge of the River Thames. Bang sent Thug Rock along with his army on this mission to ensure things ran smoothly and to be able to appropriately manage any threat that Squad Gigantic may pose.

Thug Rock and a few soldiers from Bangz Army set out to snatch the Mayor's daughter after school. The driver that was sent by the Mayor was knocked out by

Thug Rock's thunderous right hook, then whilst unconscious he was tied up and stuffed in the boot. Thug Rock took the car and waited patiently outside the school for the Mayor's daughter.

As she jumped in and settled herself, she looked around and noticed that something was wrong! When she usually got in the car her driver always played her favourite two songs of the moment and they would have a sing-a-long on the way home.

Confused to why no music was playing, The Mayor's daughter asked

"Johnny what's wrong? You always play one of our songs when I get in"

"Oh yeah, sorry... just remind me which one again" said Thug Rock attempting to disguise himself as Johnny, her usual driver.

"Durrrr, Don't act like you don't know... Hurtin' Me... Steflon Don or the Ding-a-ling song she got with Skepta" said the Mayor's daughter as she cheekily waved her hands to make a 'you should know already' gesture, as her arms swung she looked up and realised it wasn't her driver Johnny at all!

"Where's Johnny, my usual driver?" Asked the Mayor's daughter.

"He's got flu, I'm covering for him" replied Thug Rock thinking on his feet for once.

"He was fine when I saw him this morning" stated the Mayor's daughter.

"WELL HE'S NOT NOW!" Snapped Thug rock.

"Nar' he's never sick, something ain't right. I'm calling my dad" said the Mayor's daughter as she reached in her school bag and took out her phone.

Thug Rock activated the car's child lock and said "If you don't shut your mouth I'm gonna' shut it for you!" The Mayor's daughter froze.

"If you wanna' see your dad ever again... its best you shut up, pass your phone and don't make me have to talk again!" Said Thug Rock whilst throwing the drivers hat off his head.

The Mayor's daughter was scared and tears started to stream down her face. She begged Thug Rock not to hurt her and pleaded for him to let her go. Thug Rock ignored her and drove to his destination. Once he got there he dragged her up to the roof and tied her to a chair.

Thug Rock handed the Mayor's daughter her phone back and told her "Call your eediot' dad and tell him if he wants his precious baby back, it'll cost him one million pounds".

Bang didn't want the money, things we're slow but he didn't need it. He just set the ransom to raise the alarms so Squad Gigantic would be alerted and come to save her.

Things went exactly to plan to for Bang. The Mayor called the London City police (LCP) for help and Tanya picked it up on the SG System. Tanya traced the car used in the kidnap by locating it via the cities CCTV, then once she had the registration plate number she used the SG System to hack in to the car's GPS tracker. The tracker led her directly to Marlo's Shipping Co. where the car was parked outside. Once again Tanya unknowingly dispatched Squad Gigantic directly in to another one of Bang's traps.

As the teens arrived they could see Thug Rock and Bang's men on the roof.
"She's must be up there" said Safa-Rhi.

Truth huddled the team together and said "You lot, ear' what we're gonna do… me and Chunks are gonna go up from the inside".
"What if the doors are locked?" asked Pacer.

Everyone else laughed and looked at Chunksta, then Truth said "I'm sure that's not gonna be a problem… right Chunks?" Indicating that the door had no chance against Chunksta's strength.

"As soon as you two see me and Chunks up there, Pacer you come running up the side of the building and Safa-Rhi you fly up. Once I see the Mayor's daughter I'll let you know where she is. Whichever one of you can get to the Mayor's daughter first, take her to safety and we'll catch up with you after we wrap up these punks".

As predicted the door was locked, so Chunksta kicked the door of its hinges and headed for the stairs with Truth.

Thug Rock heard the smashes and loud noises from downstairs and said "Finally some action!"
The Mayor's daughter smiled and said "You better hope that's not Squad Gigantic, cos' they'll bust' your heads!"
"Is that what you think?" laughed Thug Rock as he

slowly removed his gloves to reveal his hands that are made of rock.

Everyone's eyes suddenly filled with terror as they looked at Thug Rock's hands. Even Bangz Army were scared as this was the first time they saw Thug Rock's metamorphic fists.

BOOOOMMM!!! Chunksta punched off the door to the roof and the frame surrounding it.

Truth went straight into battle kicking and punching through Bangz Army. As he ground and pounded one of Bang's soldiers he looked up and saw the Mayor's daughter getting shoved into a lock up at the back end of the roof.

Truth telepathically informed Safa-Rhi "She's being held in the lock up at the back of the roof" as Safa-Rhi summoned the Eagle to fly up.

"Let's go" commanded Safa-Rhi, as her and Pacer made their move.

Pacer got there first and shot off the lock up's lock with his lasers. Safa-Rhi followed closely behind, summoning the power of a Rhino to charge down the three soldiers surrounding the Mayor's daughter.

Truth was locked in battle at the other side of the roof. He gave one of Bang's soldiers a powerful right hook that floored him, then he put the soldier in a belly down arm lock.

Truth repeatedly asked "Who sent you? Why you take the Mayor's daughter?" trying to get answers from Bang's man.

Bang's soldier laughed and said "Are you dumb blood? It'll take a lot more than that to make me talk". Bangz Army were well seasoned mercenaries. They would die before they spoke!

Truth knew he wouldn't get any answers from him, well not from his mouth. Truth was a lot smarter than that, he was merely tricking the soldier. The only reason Truth asked the question was to get the soldier's thought process in the right place, so he could read his mind and get all the information he needed!

"IT'S A TRAP!" shouted Truth.

Then after fully reading the soldier's mind, he went on to say "Bang's trying to lure us in to see what powers we have, then he's aiming to steal our gems".

Thug Rock heard Truth shouting and he was furious, he couldn't believe that the soldier broke the Bangz Army sacred code of silence. Thug Rock lost his mind and came running towards Truth with his fist drawn back. Truth couldn't see the attack that was coming his way as he was busy putting the soldier to sleep with a submission hold. Luckily Chunksta saw Thug Rock rushing towards his brother and jumped in front of Thug Rock.

Thug Rock came to a halt and laughed saying "What you gonna do lil' man? Move before you get hurt". "You must've never heard of me G" replied Chunksta as he laughed too.

"I like your style lil' man... just for that I'll go easy on you. You set the first Bang" said Thug Rock pushing out his chin mocking Chunksta and not respecting him due to his age and height.

"Cool" said Chunksta.
"But one thing! I don't want your chin, that's too easy... I'll prefer your chest!" said Chunksta.

As Chunksta drew back and threw a powerful punch into Thug Rock's chest, Thug Rock said, "huh?" Just in time to be catapulted across the whole roof by Chunksta's mega punch. His power knocked Thug Rock out and launched him all the way into the river.

"Oops, man was going easy as well, I really don't know my own strength... oh well" said Chunksta as he continued in battle.

"Sis' you lot grab the Mayor's daughter and go... it's all a set up I'll explain later" said Truth into his sister's mind as she saw Thug Rock fly over her head into the river.

"I guess we won" said Pacer looking at Thug Rock sinking into the river.

"If we leave him in the river he'll die" said Safa-Rhi as she telepathically pleaded with her brother to save Thug Rock.

"Good, them man killed our family" Truth ruthlessly

replied.

"That's not right, we're not murderers... I'm going to save him" said Safa-Rhi.

Truth reluctantly agreed with his sister and said "Well be safe and be quick, we'll be waiting for you downstairs".

"Pacer, grab the girl and meet them lot downstairs. I'll be back in a minute" instructed Safa-Rhi.

"Say no more" responded Pacer as he took the Mayor's daughter in his arms.

As Pacer stood face to face with the Mayor's daughter, he stopped for a second as they caught eyes and he was momentarily enchanted by her beauty. Pacer shook off his trance and told the Mayor's daughter to hold on tight, then zooooommmmm! They were downstairs in a second.

Whilst Pacer was falling in love, Safa-Rhi took a run up and leaped off the building. Whilst mid-air she summoned the powers of a dolphin and elegantly dived into the river. Safa-Rhi knew Thug Rock was unconscious and if he wasn't rescued he would have no chance of surviving in the water. Thug Rock's arms being made of rock didn't help the situation at all, as they caused him to sink deeper into the river at a fast rate.

Truth and Chunksta finally got downstairs.

"You lot took your time" said Pacer showing off for the Mayor's daughter who he obviously fancied.

Truth and Chunksta looked at each other in shock then looked back at Pacer and simultaneously said "Shut

Up!".

Truth playfully slapped Pacer in the back of his head whilst he wasn't looking.
"You weren't quick enough to dodge that was you?" laughed Chunksta.

The Mayor's daughter was star struck, she totally forgot about the ordeal she had just gone through. She couldn't believe that she had just been saved by Squad Gigantic and to top it off she was spending the evening with her favourite of them all, Pacer. She didn't want Pacer to let go of her, she gripped him tight hoping the night would never end.

"Looks like you got a new girlfriend Pacer" joked Chunksta winding up his brother.
Pacer's face went red with embarrassment as he tried to hide the fact that he fancied her too.

As they laughed and joked with the Mayor's daughter, Safa-Rhi emerged from the river clutching on Thug Rock's hoodie with her teeth like how a Lion would carry its cub.
The boys made the Mayor's daughter wait behind as they walked over to Safa-Rhi. Thug Rock was still unconscious as Safa-Rhi threw him on the pier, as Thug Rock laid there lost to the World they all looked down and saw his hands.
"Rah' that's strange" said Pacer.
"No it's not" said Safa-Rhi, "It's just weird to see it here in London. Chunks, There was a family from your tribe who had hands made of rocks" continued Safa-Rhi. "I

was close with them, but I don't remember seeing him in Paradise Mountains" said Chunksta.

"Exactly he's not from there. The only time he came was when they destroyed it! I remember his face... this is crazy" said Safa-Rhi.

"He's gonna wake up soon, take some photos and send them through to Tanya and Jay. Let's get out of here" commanded Truth.

As they were leaving they walked past the car the Mayor's daughter was kidnapped in. They heard thuds coming from the boot. The boot was locked so Chunksta yanked the whole door off and was shocked to find a man tied up in there.

"That's Johnny, my driver!" said the Mayor's daughter. "Don't look like he's doing much driving in the boot" said Chunksta as he stepped back and let Johnny the driver out.

Johnny hugged the Mayor's daughter happy to see she was ok. He offered to drive her home, but Truth told him he was in no state to drive.

Truth instructed Pacer to run them both to the Mayor's residence without being seen.

Then Truth wrote up a special SG Note and gave it to Pacer, then instructed him to deliver it to the Mayor via his daughter. The SG Notes were amazing, once read it'll self-destruct into thin air ensuring that no one else could intercept the message after. The note explained to the Mayor that Bang could not be trusted and it was him who kidnapped his daughter.

As instructed Pacer dropped the Mayor's daughter

and her driver home in the blink of an eye. Although
Pacer didn't want to admit it earlier, it was clear to
see he had a crush on the Mayor's daughter. Just
before Pacer gave the Mayor's daughter the SG
Note, he gently held her hand and said
"So what's your name babes, I can't keep calling you the
Mayor's daughter forever"
"It's Angel" she replied in a shy tone.

Pacer gave her a kiss on the cheek and said
"Give this to your dad" whilst handing her the SG Note.
"You really want me to give my dad a kiss from you?"
said Angel.
"Nooo, give him the note" said Pacer in a defensive
manner.

Angel laughed at the miscommunication, then she
suddenly came to a realization and said
"I've heard this name Bang before, Marlo Bang!"

"Where?" enquired Pacer.

"I knew it, I knew that guy who kidnapped me looked
familiar!" said Angel
"That guy... your female friend just pulled out the river...
Thug Rock is what they call him. A few months ago that
man gave my dad a suitcase filled with cash, he told my
dad that if he knows what good for him he'll take the
cash and make sure Marlo Bang's name is clear for his
homecoming" said Angel.
"I knew something was dodgy, but I didn't care because
my dad took me shopping on Sloane Street straight
after and bought me a whole new wardrobe" continued

Angel.

"Thanks you don't know how you just helped me, but don't tell no one else that story and make sure your dad gets this note... even though I don't think it's gonna' be that much use!" said Pacer, then he gave her another kiss on the cheek and ran back to his brothers and sisters.

The teens got back to HQ and immediately briefed Tanya and Jay on everything that had just taken place. Sparing no details they explained how they found out it was a trap, how they discovered Thug Rock had special powers and that the Mayor accepted dirty money.

Jay realised exactly what had gone down! He was fully aware that Bang was on to the Squad Gigantic and wanted their SG Gems to complete his quest to become the most powerful man on Earth! The information Pacer received from Angel allowed Jay and Tanya to establish exactly how Bang was able to come back to London without any warrants or comebacks, Jay knew Bang was behind Swarvez death and now he also knew that the LCP and the Mayor was corrupt. The last line of defence for London and the World was Squad Gigantic!

Chapter 13.5 - Any One Can Get It!

Meanwhile, back at Marlo Shipping Co. Bang and Dealer pulled up and saw the wreckage. They found Thug Rock sitting on the pier licking his wounds.

"Oi you, GET UP!" shouted Bang to Thug Rock.
"What happened here? Actually what happened to you?" said Bang.
"It was the little one boss" said Thug Rock.

Bang and Dealer burst out laughing at Thug Rock.

"The little one done you over ands' got you sitting on the dock of the bay, who d'you think you are... Otis Reading?" said Bang.
"Who?" said Dealer and Thug Rock.
"Never mind, you idiots don't know nothing, what you need to do is tell me why my strongest fighter has been defeated by a little boy and why my business looks like a bomb hit it!" said Bang.

"He got me with a cheap shot. I didn't respect his gangsta' and he caught me slippin', that simple" replied Thug Rock.
Whilst holding his head in shame, he went on to say "Things didn't go fully to plan, we got the girl and done what you said, but that Gigantic Squad or whatever they're called were too strong."

"Wimp! Did you at least manage to see what their powers were?" said Dealer.

"Yeah all but one of them! One's fast... like real fast. Blink and you'll miss him, Usain Bolt ain't got nothing on him! The other ones got some unbelievable power and the chick could fly! The other guy, he's a fighter still' but I couldn't see what special powers he had" replied Thug Rock.

"Where's the rest of the soldiers?" asked Bang. "I think they're still on the roof, about that too..." said Thug Rock.
"What about what?" said Bang.
"Rowdy Renzo broke the code. The one without the powers had him in a submission hold and the prat spilt his guts, told him exactly what your plans were!" said Thug Rock.

Bang was fuming! He ran upstairs in a rage followed by Thug Rock and Dealer. Once upstairs they were greeted by Rowdy Renzo and a bunch of soldiers who had also been battered and bruised from the fight. Bang was disgusted and disappointed. He told them all to get up and line up at the edge of the roof... including Thug Rock! Bangz Army were about to see how ruthless Bang was and how serious he got when missions weren't executed successfully. As they all lined up on the edge of the roof, Bang explained how important loyalty was to him and why it should also be important to them.

Bang slowly walked back and forth in front of Thug Rock, Rowdy Renzo and the rest of the soldiers just to intimidate them. Bangz Army stood there whilst nervously looking down at a drop behind them which was at least four storeys down.

"See, I think I'm good to all of ya', I give you the chance to eat good, get money... loads of money actually, enough to get anything that you want in this World. You drive around in top of the range cars and you've basically got immunity out here in these mean streets of London, am I correct?" asked Bang.

"Yes sir" they replied.
"I CAN'T HEAR YA!" snapped Bang.

"YES SIR" they replied at the top of their voices. "That's better" said Bang with Dealer standing behind him with the meanest look he could pull on his face. "All I ask from you lot is professionalism and loyalty" said Bang.

Then Bang slowly walked right up to Thug Rock's face, invading his personal space and forcing Thug Rock to adjust his footing so he wouldn't fall off the edge.

"Is that correct?" said Bang as he stepped away from Thug Rock.
"YES SIR!" shouted Thug Rock, Rowdy Renzo and the rest of Bangz Army who were present.

"So why is it that I send you muppets out on a simple job to kidnap an innocent little girl and you manage to fluff it! Not only fluff it, but one of you even managed to display your disloyalty by crumbling under pressure and giving up our secrets to a teenager that had you in a little itty bitty submission hold!" Stated Bang.

"Do you fear them more than you fear me? I SAID DO

YOU FEAR THEM MORE THAN YOU FEAR ME?!" Shouted Bang in Rowdy Renzo's face.

By now Bang was livid, spit was flying out of his mouth onto the Rowdy Renzo's face. Rowdy Renzo ignored the spit and stood to attention, he knew better than to break his stance by wiping the saliva off his face so he just accepted it and allowed Bang to continue.

Bang continued to slowly pace back and forth until he got back in front of Rowdy Renzo. Then Bang calmly turned around with a smile on his face, then looked Rowdy Renzo dead in his eyes and said
"You must not fear me, I must be a joke... a real big joke! I guess I'm gonna' have to do something to prove to you that nothing's funny round 'ere mate!"

Rowdy Renzo tried to plead his case as Bang stepped closer to him.
"I ain't never been disloyal, I stand firm as a soldier and have never broke my form, my word or my loyalty to you ever!"

Bang laughed as he looked over at Dealer, then he pointed at Rowdy Renzo and said
"Oh look, now he's got heart. That's better mate, show me some passion" as he affectionately put his arm around his shoulder to reassure and comfort him.

"Calm down Rowdy, don't have a hissy fit" said Bang. Then as soon as Rowdy Renzo stood at ease and felt safe, Bang turned back around and pushed him off the roof!

The rest of the soldiers stood there shaking in their

boots hoping they weren't going to be next!

With not one ounce of emotion Bang said to the rest of the soldiers "Let that be a lesson to you all, weakness and treacherous disloyalty will not be tolerated in Bangz Army! Do you understand!?"

"YES SIR!" shouted the remaining soldiers.

"Glad I've made myself clear, now get down there and clean that mess off the floor or you'll be joining him!" commanded Bang.

Thug Rock and Bangz Army couldn't run towards the door quick enough. As they ran, Bang called out to Thug Rock
"Not you, you twat get over here!" stopping Thug Rock in his tracks.

As Thug Rock walked over to Bang, Bang said "Don't ever make me have to do that to you again, you're not one of the lackeys! Sort yourself out and don't make anything like this happen again".

"Yes boss" said Thug Rock happy he was being let off the hook. "It won't happen again. When I find that little so and so I'm gonna' knock him out!"

"I should hope so" said Dealer as they left the building.

Suddenly Bang began to feel a bit weak and unsettled, his bones were aching and he felt rather light headed so he decided to call it a night and went home to Elisha.

Bang didn't want Thug Rock and Dealer to see him weak, especially after the big statement he had just made on the roof. So he jumped in a Coupé and drove himself home.

Bang arrived home to find Elisha half asleep on the sofa. He gave her a gentle kiss on her forehead to wake her, then still hiding his pains he whispered in her ear "Come on sweetheart, its bed time".

Whilst still half asleep, Elisha got up on her feet. Bang guided her along the way as she walked to the bedroom.

"How was your day babes?" asked Elisha as she became more alert.
"Not so good luv" replied Bang.
Elisha found her focus and looked directly into his eyes and noticed he was stressed.
"You looked stressed babes, what happened?" said a concerned Elisha.
"Those plonkers messed up my plans, but I don't wanna' go into it. I'll explain everything tomorrow darling" said Bang stubbornly refusing to show Elisha he was in pain.

Bang and Elisha changed into their pyjamas and went to bed. He patiently waited for her to fall asleep. This didn't take too long as she still wasn't fully woken from her nap on the sofa.
Bang called her name twice to make sure she was sleeping, then he quietly sneaked out of the bed and went to his secret hidden safe. The hidden safe was located in the basement area of Bang's HQ which to the average eye just looked like offices connected to his

mansion. The safe was built behind a family portrait of Bang and his parents.

As he got closer to the portrait he felt his legs giving way and he fell to the ground smashing a Decanter filled with Fine French Cognac in the process. This woke Elisha up, she reached out for Bang and realised he was gone. Elisha feared the worst, half dreaming and half conscious she believed something had happened to him, she grabbed a baseball bat and slowly crept towards the basement area with the aim of confronting the intruder she thought was in the mansion.

Elisha slowly approached the area Bang was located in, Bang managed to pull himself up and access his secret safe. Elisha was shocked, all this time they've been living in this mansion Bang never showed her this secret safe, she didn't even know it was there. Once Elisha knew the suspected intruder was just Bang, she stood quietly at the door with a heart wrenching feeling of betrayal.
Without Bang noticing her she discreetly watched his every move.

Bang swung back the portrait and entered his four digit code: 0408

Elisha quickly put her phone on silent and tapped the code into her phone notes section, realising the code was the date Bang's parents were killed. Elisha then took a look over Bang's shoulders and saw directly in to the safe. The safe was filled with piles of cash, a few expensive watches and necklaces, as well as at least four passports for four different nationalities and a gun- all the usual things you would see in a high level criminal's safe. However, the main thing that caught her eyes was a clear crystal box that had a range of gems inside. These were the special gems that Bang had collected so far.

Now Elisha was riled up! She couldn't believe Bang could abuse her trust and hide all this from her. Her mind was running wild. 'What else is he hiding? If he has a secret escape pack that doesn't involve me... he must not even care about me!'

She wound herself up so much that she couldn't hold back any more. Angry and agitated she was just about to run over to Bang and let loose on him! Then she was stopped as she looked up and saw him grab the box of gems. As soon as Bang grabbed the box he fell down once again and this time his hand landed right in a thick shard of broken glass from the smashed Decanter. It was a deep cut, Bang's hand started bleeding straight away with blood gushing everywhere. Elisha put her feelings to a side and grabbed a first aid kit to tend to him. As Elisha drew nearer to Bang, he shouted and told her "Stop luv', don't worry I'll be fine". Elisha replied, "You're bleeding, stop being so stubborn".

"Trust me I'll be cool" said Bang as he placed his hands about two inches above the gems.

The gems then began to glow in a chaotic dark shade, then a cosmic force started to emerge from each gem one by one. The force was similar to the glow that Jay and Squad Gigantic's gems gave, but this force was not as blissful and free flowing as the force that was released from the SG Gems. In fact it was the total opposite.

This force was not willing to release its divine capabilities to Bang, it was as if Bang had to force the glow out as the force resisted from releasing its powers. "Stand back" said Bang protecting Elisha from what seemed like a cosmic battle between him and what he called the Dark Gems.

Eventually the force gave in to Bang and entered his body through his hand, he screamed in pain as the force entered him. Miraculously Bang's deep cut on his hand healed right there in front of Elisha's eyes, then Bang regained his strength and stood tall like a new man.

"What on Earth just happened?" said a petrified Elisha. "I never wanted you to see this" said Bang, then he went on to explain:

"With greatness there's always a cost. When I started this quest I didn't know the risk I was putting myself in, well not until I found the first Dark Gem! The spirit of the first Dark Gem I ever found spoke to me, it told me... *'You are not one of the Chosen Ones'. The force then examined my whole body and soul telling me 'You may be the evil that prophecy spoke of... the evil that wants to rule the World and bring destruction!'*
I stood there quaking in my boots and then somehow found the courage to say YES that's me.

The spirit said to me *'I can give you this dream but not only will you need to find all the other gems associated with my power, you'll also need to understand the risk and sacrifice you will personally take'*
I didn't know what it meant, but I was so hungry for the power I didn't care! I was finally close to World domination and I weren't gonna' let anything get in my way.

Then the force said, *'The force has not chosen you... you have chosen the force! So you have to draw power from the gems because the natural state doesn't accept you! This is why the power flows freely from the gems to the Chosen Ones, emitting an unlimited supply of powers and abilities as the gems respond to who they chose. Apart from the Chosen Ones, there are only two cases mentioned in the prophecy, these stories are of stones intertwining into the DNA of two unrelated orphans who will have the ability of receiving the gem's powers and acting on behalf of good or evil on a free will basis. All the gems you find on your quest will either be found at the place of the previous connected Ancient Chosen One's death or back at the mountains they originated from once the connected Ancient Chosen One died. Any other gems will have to be taken directly from the new Chosen Ones wherever they may be... but only if you are powerful enough to kill them and take the gems directly from their possession!*

For an evil spirit like yourself to acquire the powers, you will also need strength and a high pain threshold that will only come from the will you possess for being the leader of Earth! Also before you make your decision I want to make sure you clearly understand that you do not have the ability to obtain unlimited power from the gems until you acquire every last gem connected to Chosen Ones, both ancient and present.

Until then every time you draw power your natural human health and strength will be weakened as you will be battling with a cosmic force much bigger than you can imagine!'

Just before I made my decision, the force said *'The*

choice is yours. Place me back on the ground and walk away or place your hand over me and begin your new life!'
I chose not to walk away" said Bang as he stood there in a brief spell of regret.

"My health's dropped like mad luv' and if I don't continue to draw power I think imma' die!
So until I get all the remaining gems I have no choice but to continue to battle with the force from the Dark Gems every time I'm drained" said Bang.

"You won millions, you could've lived the perfect life, but you still allowed your greed to put you in this predicament?!" said Elisha with a disgusted look on her face. It was like she didn't know him anymore. From that moment something changed in how she felt towards Bang.

"I was so greedy and determined to rule the World that I ignored the healthy warning I was given and drew power from the gem. I did this for both of us! Why would you want to just own a town when we could sit on the throne of the World together like we always dreamed?" said Bang.

"No that's what you always dreamed. I just wanted a life of luxury, I didn't need the whole World! Don't you dare blame me for this mess!" responded Elisha.

"You don't complain when I bring you back jewels and gems for you and your bloody shop do ya?" said Bang.

As Bang got more and more angry, Elisha became more and more silent.

"Whether you like it or not we are in this together now luv'... you're stuck with me" said Bang. Then he walked closer to Elisha, got right up in her face then threateningly asked her "You're still with me... aren't you?!"

Elisha looked Bang back in his eyes and lied saying "Of course, I'll always stand by you".
From that moment Elisha began planning her exit route from Bang.

"Make sure you keep this between us! I know you and Dealer have become good friends over the years, but no matter how much I trust him, he can't know! No one can know or they'll wait till I'm weak and come for my crown" explained Bang.

Elisha hugged him with a cunning smile on her face, then said "Your secret's safe with me".

Elisha felt betrayed. In her mind, Bang wasn't the almighty man she thought he was.
Elisha was very materialistic and all she wanted was to be the wife of the 'man' and live a flashy life filled with jewellery, fashion, cars and all the other riches out there. Seeing Bang weak like this made her feel it was only a matter of time before he would be defeated bringing her life of luxury to an abrupt end! There was no way on Earth that she was going to allow that to happen to herself.

First thing in the morning, Elisha left the mansion on a mission. She planned to go see Dealer with the intention of bringing him round to her way of thinking! Elisha always had a slight crush on Dealer and to be honest the feeling was mutual. Although Dealer also had the mind-set of a villain, his and Bang's ways couldn't be more opposite.

Bang was a typical rough and ready manly man. He thought fashion and all the things that come with it was nonsense, he always said "That crap's for girls mate, sort yourself out Dealer".
Whereas Dealer was like Elisha. He had a deep passion for fashion, he found nothing more important than being well dressed and presentable at all times.

Dealer and Elisha would always wind up Bang over his lack of style and the way he presented himself. They would irritate Bang for hours by making fun of him and his poor dress sense. Their favourite sayings was "Bang's outfits never bang"
This would always press Bang's buttons the wrong way, then he would get mad and tell them to get lost.

As time went by Elisha and Dealer got closer, but with Bang being so focused on his quest he was oblivious to it all. Everyone except Bang could see the chemistry between the two, but luckily for Bang the both of them were too loyal to him to actually act upon it.

Thug Rock wasn't the sharpest tool in the box, but even he could see there was something deeper going on between Elisha and Dealer. Thug Rock was forever giving warnings to Dealer saying
"You're playing a risky game bro, you and Elisha are looking real close".
Dealer would always laugh it off and profess his

innocence alongside declaring his loyalty to Bang.

Unfortunately for Bang, Elisha's thoughts had now changed which was bound to have a dangerous outcome to their relationship. Elisha was on a quest of her own! Her main aim in life was simply to live a life of luxury and be the wife of the Boss. After Bang exposed her to the truth behind his reign, she now looked at Dealer as the next one to be in power if and when Bang falls from his grace.

However for Elisha's plan to run smoothly, she would need Dealer's love to protect her from any retaliation Bang may seek. So with this in mind she made a surprise visit to Dealer at the Ace Of Clubs as he prepared for the nights under 18's rave.

As always Dealer greeted Elisha with a kiss on each cheek, he then asked her to wait for him in his office as he tied up a few loose ends. Elisha sat at Dealer's desk with a conniving grin on her face. Sitting in his chair made her feel powerful and in control. In front of her was a massive one way glass window which gave her a perfect view of the club. Elisha sat there and gazed through this window as she fantasised about being Dealer's partner and ruling the empire together. Elisha's day dream was interrupted by Dealer as he walked in with a black bottle of Champagne and two crystal flute glasses.
Elisha looked at him and smiled, then said "I could get use to this" gently flirting with Dealer.

Elisha and Dealer spoke for over an hour. She told him all about the incident that took place with Bang the night before. She informed Dealer of how weak Bang was without the Dark Gems and repeated the whole story that Bang explained to her about ascertaining the first Dark Gem. Elisha literally told Dealer everything she knew, even though she swore to Bang that she would keep it a secret. Dealer also heard mention of the two orphans in the story that was relayed to him. Immediately he knew it referred to him and Thug Rock, but he decided to keep quiet on the matter.

With the hope of planting a thought process into Dealer's mind that would cause separation between him and Bang, Elisha went on to manipulate his mind even more! She stroked his ego by telling Dealer that he should be the leader.

"Bang's half the man you are, think about it babes. Anytime something needs sorting out who has to do it? You and Thug Rock! Not Bang, he just pulls up at the end and starts playing the big man once all the hard works done! As for Thug Rock, he's cool and everything, but we know he's all muscle and no brains, he'll be nothing without your lead! You're the true leader of the gang!" said Elisha.

Elisha's plan to manipulate Dealer was working. All the information she gave him about Bang made him question Bang's loyalty to him and Thug Rock. Elisha used the perfect blend of truth with lies to put loads of doubt in Dealer's mind.

Her mind was set. She was ready to leave Bang and be with Dealer! The only problem was that even though Dealer was beginning to have second thoughts about Bang, his loyalty was overpowering the doubts he had regarding his boss.

Elisha saw it wasn't going to be easy to persuade Dealer, so she decided to up her levels. As they finished talking, she slowly leaned in and gave Dealer a pressing hug and gently whispered in his ear.
"From the first day I met you, I knew I should've chose you" then she kissed him on the cheek and slowly walked out of the room.

Dealer stood there gobsmacked as he watched her leave, he couldn't believe what Elisha just whispered in his ear. He always knew they had feelings for each other but none of them ever spoke on it. His mind started to wonder, he couldn't help but think about how great it would be to have Elisha as his girlfriend and what it would be like if he was the leader.

Then Dealer thought to himself 'For real, she has a point! It's me and Thug Rock that does all the hard work, Bang wouldn't be nothing without us... nothing but a frail man clutching on to those stupid gems. Elisha's right, he ain't fit to be the man. One wrong move and I'm taking the throne... and his Queen!'

Elisha's plan had worked, now she had Dealer's full attention!

Chapter 14 - Who Don't Hear Must Feel!

When Bang woke up his house was empty, but he was refreshed and full of drive. He decided the time was now, he was done playing games... it was time to take out Squad Gigantic!

Bang got himself washed and dressed then went to see his tech guy 'Mechanics'. Mechanics had a car repairs garage on the outskirts of London in a town called Crawley. This location was perfect as he was right next to the city's major airport, so he could import and export whatever he wanted nice and easy. Bang and Mechanic's relationship stretched back years. Mechanics was his weapons guy and he could get his hands on nearly anything!
Mechanics also done all Bang's tech related jobs, he designed the Bangz Army armour, manufactured the Gem Tracker and basically completed any tech related task alongside computer and systems hacking.
Mechanic's car repair garage was just a front and round the back was where all the action really took place, it was a weapon haven for the underworld. If Mechanics liked you, he had the ability to supply you with anything from handguns to Alien tech weaponry... for the right price.
After being informed of all the powers and abilities

Squad Gigantic possessed, Bang wanted to make sure he was fully equipped to deal with the threat they posed.

"Mr Bang, long time no see my friend. I miss you aye geezer" said Mechanics with his comical accent. Mechanics and his family migrated from Italy to the UK when he was around twelve years old. Mechanics grew up in East London around cockney gangsters and this made him speak in a crazy tongue which derived from a cockney slang combined with an Italian accent, it was the funniest thing ever.

"Missed you too pal, you and that stupid accent" laughed Bang.
"Ladies love-a the way-a I talk matey, so shut-a your face" replied Mechanics.

Bang and Mechanics relationship was full of banter. In fact Mechanics was probably the only person who could tell Bang to shut up and get away with it, they were that good of friends.

"Anyway I'm not here for your stand up show mate, I'm here on business. I got a little problem I need to take care of! I know... well I think you're the perfect man to help me solve it" said Bang.

"Spit it out amico, I'm a very busy uomo pal" said Mechanics as they walked to the back of the workshop.

"You're a what? You don't half talk rubbish mate. But anyway, I'm up against something I've never gone against before mate. In a nutshell I need weapons and armour to go against a gang that's ultra powerful, ultra fast, shoots out bloody lasers and one even has the ability to fly!"

Mechanics started to frantically wave his hands about shouting "Mama Mia, that sounds like-a some-a heavy stuff mate".
Then he put his hand on Bang's shoulder and said "Let's go in-a to-a the secret secret room".

"I thought this was the secret room mate" said Bang.

"Ohhh noo matey, I ha-ve-ra special place for stuff this-a heavy" said Mechanics as he led Bang towards a solid brick wall.
Mechanics placed his hand dead in the centre of the wall, then the solid brick transformed into a scanner and scanned his retinas.

"Welcome sir" said the room's security system in the most soft inviting voice you ever heard. As Bang followed Mechanics into the room the lights switched to red, a force field trap formed around Bang and isolated him to a space no bigger than a squared metre. The force field then formed two small gaps, with each one no bigger than an inch. Two Machines Guns then ejected out of the ceiling and their nozzles slotted perfectly into these gaps. Bang feared for his life as he stood there helpless with the guns pointing directly at his face.

The security systems tone of voice changed to a stern one and warned Bang "Intruder you have precisely 10 seconds to identify yourself or you will be terminated".

Bang stood dead still filled with fear, then he tried to
identify himself whilst begging Mechanics to save him.
"Bang, my name's Bang. Oi Mechanics, what's going on!
Don't just stand there... help me!".
"Oh my days-a, I forgot bout that hahahahahahaha"
laughed Mechanics but Bang didn't find it funny at all!
The system continued counting down "8..7..6".
"Well bloody do something!" shouted Bang becoming
more worried as Mechanics just laughed.

Bang tried to move his body up and down to get
himself out of the Machine Gun's range, but whenever
he moved, the Gun's nozzles simply adjusted and
followed him. The system was about to unload its
bullets on Bang, then with just two seconds left,
Mechanics pressed a combination of digits to give Bang
clearance and grant him access. The guns retracted back
in to the ceiling and the force field disappeared. As the
lighting went back to normal the system then said in its
calm soothing voice "Welcome visitor".

Mechanics continued to laugh at Bang's reaction and he
spurted out "That was close aye pal, almost-a lost ya
hahahahahahaha".

Bang wasn't amused!

Mechanics eventually managed to contain his laughter.
"Ok, ok... whoo let's get-a serious again. Firstly you
sound like-a you are fighting super heroes matey, so
you need-a a super villain suit huh" said Mechanics.

"I have-a the perfect thing for you geezer" said

Mechanics as he pressed a button that released a hidden compartment from the floor. Bang jumped to the left as the piece of the floor he was standing on started to rise up.

A big transparent capsule eventually emerged from the ground and revealed a suit that was literally from out of this World. The suit was blue with touches of black, it was beautiful.

"The material-a... it-a looks kinda like-a leather aye geezer, but nooo' it's-a crazy material... top of-a the range! I don't even have a name for it bruv! It's-a some-a sort-a alien technology!" said Mechanics slapping Bang in his chest out of excitement. "This-a bad boy can take an atomic blast bruv'... well maybe not... but almost. What I'm-a sayin' is, you wear this-a whistle and flute... ain't nobody-a troubling you geezer" said Mechanics boasting about his product.

Bang stood in awe, the suit was perfect!
"How many of them have you got?" asked Bang.
"Not a lot mate, these-a bad boys are exclusive... so exclusive mate you can only-a get them in space hahahahahahaha" laughed Mechanics.
"Funny mate, but serious how many and how much?" said a serious Bang.
"Ok ok, keep- ya shirt on mate. I've only got one, that's all that was-a recovered. Let me do a few-a minor tweaks and-a put a nice 'B' for Bang aye, then I give you it for £2million" said Mechanics.

"Done" said Bang.
Then Bang went on to say "That sorts out the laser and

blast crap, but what about the speed and flying malarkey?"

"Have a look over here mate, I call this-a one a Soul Freezer... doesn't matter how-a fast or-a strong you are mate, when this hits you... you ain't-a going no where! Its-a got three functions: Freeze shots to freeze stun a lil' so and so, Burn shots what-a burns to kill or Grenade launcher to blow up-a everybody hahahaha. Crazy aye? Has a range of at least 50 metres buddy! I only-a made two of these-a babies... nobody else in the World got one geezer" said Mechanics gleaming with joy.

Bang heard all he needed to hear and quickly said "How much they cost?" as if he was afraid someone else would take them.
"Let's-a say £2million for the suit and-a £500k for the Soul Freezers" said Mechanics starting the negotiations "Throw in some extra armour for the army with some ammo and I'll take it" said Bang.
"It's a deal, I'll-a even throw in some Tranquilizer Guns too matey... that should-a slow the fast guy down hahahaha... just cos' I love ya geezer... just cos' I love ya" said Mechanics.
"They'll be at your-a place before you get there mate" said Mechanics as he sealed the deal with a wink.
"Perfect, I don't wanna' get pulled over by the coppers with a bloomin' alien gun... they'll never let me go" joked Bang.
"I'll have my accountant wire you the dosh from one of my off shore accounts" said Bang. "Nessun problema geezer" said Mechanics.
"As always, it's been a pleasure doing business with you mate... just sort out that security rubbish" said Bang as

he left and jumped into his blacked out 4x4.

Bang left Mechanic's place feeling good, he was now ready to battle!

Meanwhile back in London, Squad Gigantic were feeling good too... probably a bit too good! They felt excited over defeating Thug Rock and Bangz Army. Previously they took on loads of Bangz Army to stop crimes, but this was their first real battle against Thug Rock, one of Bang's main men- one who also had super powers too. The Squad felt invincible, they were ready to take on the World.

Jay brought the Squad back to reality with some blunt and harsh words. "Don't get to excited, you beat up a couple of Bang's sen' out boys and yeah you sent the Rock hand yout' for a swim, but he gave you a free shot! Next time he won't give you a chance, they'll be coming at you full force! If you get arrogant, you may not be so lucky next time".

The teens were quite disheartened by these words, they felt they deserved more credit than what Jay was giving them. They'd been breaking their backs day in day out as London city heroes and haven't received any real thanks or appreciation.

The teens made up their minds and decided that they deserved to let their hair down. They grouped together to ask Jay if they could go to a party that night, they had a feeling Jay would say no but thought it was worth a try.

The teens sent Safa-Rhi and Chunksta to ask, hoping Jay would be charmed by the female and youngest sibling… unfortunately, that didn't work.

"Jay, I know it's technically a school night… but it is Thursday so the week's basically done. Also, you know how well we've all been doing at school and all that…" said Safa-Rhi with the sweetest voice ever. "…And even been saving the World" added Chunksta with a pathetic attempt to soften his deep voice.

Jay was sat in his office, as they spoke he slowly placed the document he was reading on his desk. He then looked up at Safa-Rhi and Chunksta saying "Get to the point, what are you asking for? And furthermore before you say anything else, it better not be about that party over at Ace of Clubs tonight!"

"Arrgggghhh, pleaeeaaassssee" begged Safa-Rhi. "Everyone's gonna' be there and we don't ever ask for anything really" continued Safa-Rhi.
"That's because you have everything already. You're not exactly living a hard life are ya'" replied Jay. "I know and we love you for that, but we've been working real hard recently and we just wanna' go and have a lil' bit of fun" pleaded Safa-Rhi.

"I get what you're saying luv' and you're right it's been a crazy time for us all, but to be honest it's just the beginning, Bang's here on a serious mission and things are only gonna' get worst. This ain't a time to be letting your hair down and losing your discipline. Now's the time to be more focused than ever, you can't afford to get caught slippin'" said Jay.

"We'll be extra careful and we don't ever go anywhere

without our SG Watches, and…".

Jay interrupted her, screwed his face up and then said "And hold on, to make it worst it's a school night! What type of idiots do a under 18 rave on school night! You lot ain't going nowhere! I don't even know why I'm explaining myself, like I'm not the adult here! No means no so come outta' my face and stop bothering me, I'm doing something" said Jay.

Safa-Rhi and Chunksta were defeated, they huffed in frustration and walked out of Jay's study. As they reached the passage, Chunksta looked at his sister and said "I don't know bout' you lot but I'm going out tonight!" "How? Jay said no" said Safa-Rhi.

"So, look at the size of this house… is he really gonna' notice if we're gone?" Asked Chunksta.

"You know what, you might be right. Ain't Jay and Tanya out at that charity event tonight anyway!?" said Safa-Rhi.

"Oh yeah! See I'm gone. As soon as they go out I'm hitting the roads… you rolling?" said Chunksta raising his eyebrows with a cheeky grin.

"Let's see what the others are saying first bro" cautiously replied Safa-Rhi.

Safa-Rhi and Chunksta ran upstairs to find Truth and Pacer playing computer. Chunksta pushed the power button on the console bringing the game to an abrupt end.

"What you doing you fool? You're always playing!" said Pacer.

"Shut up man I got sutum' to tell you" said Chunksta.

Totally forgetting what his little brother just did Pacer

said "What did Jay say yes? No way!"

"Nar he weren't having none of it! But I got a plan- we can creep out when him and Tanya go to that ting' tonight. We just gotta get back before they do and they won't know a thing" said Chunksta trying to convince his brothers.

"Nar I'm not on it!"

"If Jay said no it's a NO! He'll have his reasons and we need to respect that" said an adamant Truth understanding the seriousness of what was happening between them and Bang.

"You are so boring, lighten up man" said Safa-Rhi to her twin.

"No you lot need to smarten up and stop acting like some little spoilt brats" replied Truth.

Then Truth telepathically spoke into Safa-Rhi's mind "Don't you remember what happened the last time we disobeyed our parents?"

Safa-Rhi had no response to Truth's words and the conversation stopped there, Truth walked off whilst the others stayed in the living room.

"As I said, I'm going! If he don't wanna' reach that's his business. What you lot sayin'... you still on it?" Said Chunksta extending the offer for a final time.

"Yeah let's do it" said Pacer with Safa-Rhi also nodding her head in agreement.

"Jay should be gone by 8 or 8:30 the latest, so be ready by 9 and then we party baby" said Safa-Rhi whilst doing a little dance.

The clock finally struck 9pm. As planned, Jay and Tanya were long gone, by now they were most likely sipping champagne and eating a three course meal.

"Jay's gone but what about Truth, he ain't gonna let us go" complained Chunksta.
"Don't worry I got a plan... watch this" said Pacer with a devious look on his face.

Pacer was dressed way before the others as he was excited because he knew Angel would be attending the party. He slicked back his hair with half a tub of gel and drowned himself in aftershave. Pacer wore a white designer shirt with a blue finish, a soft pair of fitted jeans and his smart designer brand trainers. This was his favourite outfit and as far as he was concerned, he looked so good that there was no way Angel could resist him. However, there was one issue that Safa-Rhi had to bring up and unfortunately burst Pacer's bubble with. Angel doesn't actually know Danny... she knows Pacer, he can't talk to her about their previous encounter as it would expose his hidden identity! Pacer still as confident as ever refused to be defeated and decided that tonight was the night he makes Angel fall for Danny!

Pacer quickly ran to check on Truth's whereabouts. Truth was in his room listening to the rapper Stormzy's new album with headphones on. Pacer got in and out of his room in a few split seconds whilst managing to take Truth's bedroom door key. Without Truth noticing a thing, Pacer swiftly locked Truth in his room from the outside.

Truth was disrupted by the sound of his door slamming and jumped up only to find out he had been locked in his room. Safa-Rhi and Chunksta were waiting for Pacer in the passage with their party outfits on. Safa-Rhi wore a black and red designer jump suit with matching red bottom shoes. Chunksta never had time for all the dressing up malarkey. He always said 'the flashy tings' long'', so he just threw on a black hooded tracksuit and a fresh pair of trainers.

"Quick... hurry up and run before he gets out" shouted Pacer as he laughed and zoomed pass them. They grabbed their bits and ran straight out of the house cracking up with laughter as Truth was banging on his door shouting, "OPEN THE DOOR YOU LITTLE DOUGHNUTS!".

Truth was shouting and pounding on his door in vain, as by now they had all left the house. However Truth didn't think they would be brave enough to really lock him in and go out, so he sat for at least an hour chilling and listening to music thinking they will soon stop with the silly games and unlock his door.

Time passed and Truth realised they were not coming back! He picked up his phone and typed in how to pick a lock, within seconds he escaped his room.

Meanwhile, the rest of the teens were having a great time at the Ace of Clubs. Truth sent Safa-Rhi a constant barrage of telepathic messages informing her of what he was going to do to each one of his siblings when he catches up with them. Safa-Rhi purposely ignored her twin and this wound him up even more!

As the night went on Safa-Rhi started to feel guilty.

She separated herself from the party and chilled on a sofa regretting the decision she made. As she sat there, Pacer came over to see what was wrong.

"Yo sis, wha gwarn' why you sitting here all lonely and that?" Asked Pacer.

"I'm surprised you even notice, you ain't moved from that Angel chick all night" replied Safa-Rhi with a little giggle.

"Louw' me man, it ain't easy but somebody gotta' do it... big and serious tho' she ain't having it! Keeps lying to man... sayin' she goes out with Pacer! She's even telling me I'm trying to copy his trim and all that... the way I wanna' slap her and tell her stop frontin'... I'm Pacer!" said Pacer in a frustrated tone.

"But don't worry bout' all that, my game will work soon... but for real tho' sis what's up?" asked Pacer.

"Nothing I'm cool, well actually... I feel kinda' bad, I don't think we should've disrespected Jay and left Truth like that" said Safa-Rhi full of regret.

"He'll be cool man... what has he been cussing you?" said Pacer with the biggest grin on his face.

Safa-Rhi simply replied "Yep"

"Don't watch that sis, he'll get over it" said Pacer.

As they spoke the crowd starting rushing towards the stage.

"Cheer up sis, come we go see what's going on over there" said Pacer as he dragged his sister by the arm and pulled her towards the stage.

When they got to the front they looked up and saw

Chunksta on the stage rapping. Chunksta had the whole crowd going crazy with his lyrics. The teens couldn't believe it, they didn't even know Chunksta could rap so well.

Chunksta's lyrics:
"I grab mics and I buss' em' up standardly

Just like how I buss' up man for my family

Things change since the day them Grabberz ran from me

You hear me screaming ITS ON you better run homie

I can do it in the one up

I can do it with my fam

So if a boy try run up all he's gonna get is bangs

I'll come thru one up and rip up your whole gang

I'm biggest bad man... no matter how short I am!

What you want more... Yo DJ Ceesix stop the riddim' G

I'm g'd up from the feet up if anyone got a problem...

Speak up

I'll creep up...... with the heat tucked.....

In a blacked out trackie wid' a hoodied' top

Like who's sayin what!?!"

Chunksta was amped up and feeling himself so much that he called his brother and sister on the stage... this was a big mistake! The Squad Gigantic teens didn't know that Ace Of Clubs was owned by one of their

biggest enemies... Dealer!
Dealer, Thug Rock and a few of Bang's soldiers were chilling in the office with the large one way window that looked over the dance floor.

"Yo what's going on down there?" said Dealer as the crowd ran towards the stage.
Thug Rock walked over to the window and laughed saying "It must be Christmas bro".

"Why?" said Dealer.
"Look who it is. That's those Squad Gigantic youts'... well, all but one I think. This is a gift from the Gods bro" said Thug Rock.

"No way" said Dealer.
"Yes way bro, look at them. Obviously they ain't got on their fancy suits but look em' in the face" said Thug Rock forgetting that Dealer hasn't seen them face to face since they were children in Paradise Mountains.

"That's the little so and so that sucker punched me" said an embarrassed Thug Rock as Dealer and the others mocked him saying "Who the little one hahaha, sort it out mate... you should be ashamed to even say that".

"Alright, Alright! You gonna' stop laughing at me and give Bang a call" said Thug Rock.
"Nar, you know he's gonna' say some foolishness, I got a plan! Let's grab those Tranquilliser Guns that Bang's homie sent earlier, then go downstairs and ever so discreetly hit em', then we bring them to Bang as a present" said Dealer.

"Why use the tranquillisers, and not the real ones" said Thug Rock.
"Cos' that will kill them dummy. If we kill them Bang will never get what he wants… dead mouths don't speak" replied Dealer.

Thug rock eventually made sense of what Dealer explained to him and said "Let's do it". Then they all left the room to go action the plan.

Back at the Squad Gigantic household, Truth was fuming! He weren't going to let his siblings disrespect slide, he decided he was going to the rave and dragging them out! He grabbed his helmet and jumped on his SG1000 Super Bike! Ignoring the Highway Code, he sped all the way down to the Ace Of Clubs without stopping for any of the red lights. Truth arrived at the club just in time, not knowing he was about to walk into the biggest battle of his life!

Chapter 15 - Let's Do This!

The club was still buzzing and the party was nice, it was one of the most packed nights the Ace Of Clubs had ever seen. This was perfect for Truth as well as Thug Rock and Dealer who crazily all had the same idea, just with different intentions. Truth aimed to sneak up on Pacer so he didn't have a chance to run, however Thug Rock and Dealer were thinking the exact same thing... just for a totally different purpose!

Thug Rock and Dealer walked through the club towards Pacer, Chunksta and Safa-Rhi. Whilst walking, they discreetly held the Tranquilliser Guns down by their sides as they didn't want to create a scene when they took the teens.

As Truth crept through the dance floor and got closer to his siblings, Thug Rock and Dealer were coming from the opposite angle and they were even closer. Truth was just about to approach Pacer, then something made him look up and at that exact moment Dealer shot Pacer from point blank range with a Tranquilliser Dart. At the exact same time Thug Rock and one of Bang's soldiers simultaneously shot Safa-Rhi and Chunksta with the other Tranquilliser Guns.

Truth was about to engage them in battle, then all of a sudden he had a horrible vision of him coming under attack and drastically losing the fight, then being carried away with his sedated siblings! The vision also showed loads of innocent party goers being collateral damage! This was the first time he ever had a vision and it felt so real that he couldn't ignore it, it was as if he predicted a possible future.

Shaken by the negative result of his vision, Truth decided it would be silly for him to attack as he was outnumbered and outgunned. So rather than put himself and the others at even more risk, Truth quickly evaluated the situation and came to the conclusion that Bang's men didn't want to cause them serious harm or they wouldn't have tranquillised them. Taking slight comfort from his evaluations, Truth fell back in to the shadows and watched as Thug Rock, Dealer and Bangz Army carried his siblings out of the club disguising them as drunk party attendees that needed to be thrown out.

The teens were thrown into the back of a van which sped off down the high street towards one of Bang's secret lock ups on the docks. Truth suited up and jumped on his SG1000, he activated his bike's stealth mode and followed the van in deep pursuit. Whilst riding, Truth tried to telepathically communicate with his sister, but he wasn't successful as she was still unconscious in the back of the van.

Truth saw exactly where Bang's men took his siblings. As he arrived he saw Bang pull up followed by an army convoy of Bang's soldiers. Truth counted what looked like at least one hundred men and then skrrrrr'd' back to the Squad Gigantic HQ for help, knowing he couldn't do this on his own. Truth's calm and quick thinking allowed him to be led straight to Bang and also prevent Squad Gigantic's true identities being exposed to the public, but at the same time Truth's intelligence allowed him to know that they were severely out numbered and was about to fight a losing battle even if Jay was standing by his side.

On his way back to HQ Truth sent an emergency distress call out to Jay and Tanya. Jay and Tanya recovered the call and immediately returned to HQ to find out exactly what was going on. Truth quickly explained the situation at hand to his parents, then gave them the location of where his brothers and sister were being held captive.

Jay was upset they disobeyed his order, but there was now a bigger problem at hand. The teens needed saving and to make the situation worse, Bang was unknowingly in the same facility as three of the SG Gems which he needed to rule the World!

Jay, Truth and Tanya ran down to the hideout in the basement to load up with gadgets and tools. As they loaded up, Jay looked at Tanya and Truth then said "I've got something to show you both, Truth I'm surprised you didn't know already".
"What?" said Tanya.

Then Truth went on to say "I never use my powers on you and I never will, you're a father to me".
Truth was really worried about his siblings and when he was worried he became emotional and always revealed his true feelings to his close ones.

Tanya was pressing loads of buttons on the SG System to see if she could get a response from the teens and their suits, but the communications were still down indicating that the squad were still tranquillised. Tanya eventually stopped pressing buttons, raised her eyebrows and looked up at Jay then said

"Well show us then!"

Then with the biggest smile on his face Jay stood tall and slowly his upper body started to transform!

First it was his arms, both his muscles and veins started popping out. Jay was well built already but now his arms were monstrous! Adding to this a black fur started forming over the muscles and veins, then Jay's canine teeth started to grow bigger and his eyes went red. The black fur spread even more and now Jay's whole upper body and face transformed in to a Black Lion!

"What the...!" shouted Truth.

"This is amazing" said Tanya, then she stroked Jay's new Lion like face and asked him "Does it hurt babes?" Even though she was astonished by Jay's transformation she was still concerned for her husband's wellbeing.

"Not at all babes, it actually feels kinda good! I can feel a strength I've never felt before and I've got the ability to move and do things I never ever could do... I've got special powers too!" said Jay as he threw his hands in the air and let out a powerful roar!

"I assume it all started when I got bit by that Black Lion in Paradise Mountains, ever since that day I felt slight changes but I didn't want to mention it just in case it all went wrong and I became evil or something! So I stayed patient and gave it time, then eventually I fully transformed and learned how to control this gift I've been given" explained Jay.

"That why you're always at training at least an hour before us all ain't it?" said Truth making sense of Jay's revelation.

"Yep, we've all been in intensive training" replied Jay.

"So why didn't show us before" said Tanya.

"As I said I weren't sure what would come of it and on top of that, I wanted to save it for a day it was really needed... like now" replied Jay as he loaded up and jumped on to his super charged SG Quad Bike.

"That's all good big man, but I'll be honest... I counted at least 100 men as well as Thug Rock, Bang and the other guy! Just your new powers and mine combined won't be enough!" said Truth.

Then Tanya smiled and said "Don't worry, you lot ain't the only ones with tricks up your sleeves".

Jay was baffled, he looked at her full of excitement and said "You got powers too?"

"Don't be silly, how would I have powers I'm from London" said Tanya.

Jay was a little disappointed and said "I'm from London too... so what you got to show us then?"

As Jay spoke, Tanya pressed a special button on the system and within seconds the hide out's secret outer door opened. Jay and Truth jumped off their bikes and stood in a defensive stance ready to fight thinking Bangz Army had found the location to their HQ and breached the doors.

"Relax" said Tanya as the door opened fully.
"I'm not just a pretty face, here's something me and Mummy G have been putting together since Squad Gigantic was formed. Jay... Truth, come outside and meet the SG Hit Squad!"

The SG Hit Squad was secretly put together by Mummy G and Tanya. Mummy G knew a day would come when Squad Gigantic would need a team to take on major forces and threats. So when Jay allowed the teens to use their powers and become super heroes, she made contact with what was left of the Paradise Mountains. She got through to the current leader who offered the services of himself and only nine other warriors. The Paradise Mountains were hit really hard by Bang's attack and that was all the warriors available. Knowing ten warriors wouldn't be enough, Mummy G reached out to Tanya who then contacted a few of her special agent connections from her days as a tech specialist at the MOD. After intense scrutiny and background checks, these soldiers were accepted into the SG Hit Squad and pledged their allegiance to Tanya, Paradise Mountains and Squad Gigantic anytime they needed to be called on.

Jay and Truth stepped out to see at least twenty warriors in all black uniforms with the SG symbol on their chest and face masks. As they stood there analysing the situation, the leader of the SG Hit Squad slowly walked towards Jay.

"No way, it can't be?!?" said Jay filling with shock, emotion and joy all at the same time.

The leader of the SG Hit Squad was none other than Santago! Chief Danjuma's right hand man.

Jay went back to human form then grabbed Santago's hand and said "I thought you was dead, when... HOW? I saw them... you were outnumbered... I saw them!" Jay was confused and overwhelmed, he couldn't believe his eyes.

"It's take a lot more than that to get rid of me Jay. When you got away the Mountains were left in a bad way but it was not destroyed. The few people we have left from each tribe have been rebuilding it back to its true glory and although we have a long way to go, we will get there one day" said Santago.

Jay was bedazzled as he tried to take in everything Santago told him.

Suddenly Jay caught himself and shouted "Grandad... where's Grandad is he here?"

Santago looked down at the ground, shook his head then said "No, unfortunately Chief Danjuma is not with us".

Jay's heart fell, it was like he was given a false hope that was snatched right back from him.

"Anyway Jay, enough of the sentimental stuff. From what I hear we've got some Chosen Ones to save".

Jay and Santago discussed their plan of action, they decided Tanya was to stay back at HQ to run the comms whilst Jay, Truth and the SG Hit Squad rolled out.

Jay led on his SG Quad Bike followed by Truth on his SG1000. The SG Hit Squad followed behind in the SG Hit

Squad Truck... now Squad Gigantic had their own convoy.

The SG Hit Squad didn't have as much numbers as Bangz Army but what they lacked in numbers they made up for in skill and bravery, it was a true case of quality over quantity.

Chapter 16 - A Drop Of Rain...

Finally the teens regained consciousness. They woke up confused and disoriented in an abandoned warehouse tied up and surrounded by Bang and his army. Bang was ready for battle, he was dressed for the occasion in his new suit with his Soul Freezer Gun gripped tight in his right arm.

Pacer tried to run but it was useless as he was tied to a chair which was bolted down to the ground. His arms were also pointing towards the floor so he couldn't activate his suit and gain access to his lasers. Chunksta used his power to rip off his chains then he launched towards Dealer! Chunksta was close to making contact with Dealer then...POOOWWWW!!!! Bang shot Chunksta with the Soul Freezer, using the Freeze function he temporarily froze Chunksta.

"He's a feisty one him, better keep him one ice! Hahahahaha" said Bang. It was the first time he used the Soul Freezer on someone and he loved it!

Safa-Rhi decided the best way to play it was cool, so rather than fight she decided to communicate with her brother.
"Bro we're in trouble, I'm not sure where we are but Bang and his gang caught us slippin'" said Safa-Rhi directly speaking in to her brother's mind.

Happy to be back in contact with his sister, Truth

smiled then replied

"Don't worry sis you lot be patient and stand firm, I know what's going on and exactly where you are... we're on our way now!" Truth was relieved, hearing from his sister lifted a huge weight off his chest.

"Jay I've made contact" said Truth through his comms.
"Tell them to activate their suits so we can all communicate" replied Jay.

"Sis activate your suits so we can all speak" said Truth to Safa-Rhi.
"I can't, both me and Pacer are tied up and Chunksta's on ice" said Safa-Rhi.
"On ice?" said Truth.
"You'll see when you get here. He's ok... I think, but he's literally frozen in ice" replied Safa-Rhi.

"Ok, I need you to tell me how we can get in" said Truth.
"They've got every entrance guarded, the only thing I can suggest is brut force or creating a diversion on the south of the building then invading the north... sut'um' like that" suggested Safa-Rhi.
"No probs sis, just hold tight... soon come" said Truth.

Now that Safa-Rhi and Pacer were awake, Bang decided it was time to start the interrogations.
"You lot have caused a lot of trouble round 'ere for me and ma' goons. Really and truly I should point this beautiful piece of machinery that I've got right here directly at your pretty little face and obliterate you!"
Then Bang grabbed Safa-Rhi's face by her cheeks and shouted "SHOULDN'T I!!!!"

Rather than reply to Bang, Safa-Rhi stayed silent and telepathically told Truth to hurry up instead.

"No more games, you got 10 seconds to tell me where all your gems are or I'm gonna' slowly torture you all and then... when I finally get bored of causing you excruciating pain... I'll be kind enough to kill you!" threatened Bang.

Both Pacer and Safa-Rhi stayed silent. Luckily the SG Gems were hidden well in the SG Watches or Bang would've seen them and snatched them from the teens there and then.

Bang was so close but still so far as he didn't realise that three of the gems were actually in the same room as him!

"I admire your silence, I really do. Just the other day I had to get rid of one of my soldiers as he didn't demonstrate the same ability to keep quiet under pressure like you both are, but carry this on and I'll send you to meet him! Now you got 5 secs or your brother that's over there on ice is gonna' get it first!"

"Stop talking Rubbish and do your thing big man, if you're gonna' kill us... get on with it! You know as well as I know you need us to get to them gems! Untie us and fight like a man, if you win we'll take you to the gems fam'" said Pacer In an audacious manner.

"Hahahaha... look at this, we got a little tuff' nut ere'. You a little bad boy yeah, Ohhh look at me gangster

gangster" said Bang whilst waving his hands around mocking Pacer.

"You play a little bit of grime music in your house now you think you're hard ennit, you put on a deep voice and say some tuff' words and now you think you're Skrapz! Well let me tell you something you little twat, I've forgotten more things about the streets than you will ever know. You're not a bad boy! But have this as a gentle reminder of it all" said Bang, then he clinched his fist and punched Pacer in his jaw.

"Now every time you're about to play bad boy, just remember my fist knocking the sense outta' your north and south" laughed Bang.

"Touch him again and watch!" Shouted Safa-Rhi in defence of her little brother.

"Watch what sweetheart, what's a cute little girl like you gonna do aye'?" said Bang not taking one ounce of Safa-Rhi serious.

"You lot are way to gobby for my liking! I'm done with all the games. I tried to be Mr Nice Guy, so I guess it's time to see Mr Nasty instead!" said Bang as he walked over to a massive lever in the wall.

Bang commanded Thug Rock and Dealer to drag Safa-Rhi and Pacer over to where he was standing. As they arrived Bang pulled the lever down and the floor slowly opened up. As the floor opened a dark black pit appeared.

Bang started laughing saying, "You two still feeling hard?" He waited for a response but the teens stayed silent.

"I thought not" said Bang then he told everyone to be quiet and took a £2 coin out of his pocket.

Bang tossed the £2 coin into the dark black pit looking down at it until it was out of sight. After at least ten seconds of complete silence Bang looked up at everyone and said
"Did you hear that?" Everyone looked around confused as there wasn't a sound.
"Exactly, neither did I hahahaha that's cos' there was no sound! Quick science lesson, In order for that £2 coin to make a sound it would've had to of landed and hit the floor. Now that's gonna' be a bit hard to do or hear in a bottomless pit... COS THERE AIN'T NO FLOOR!!! If you're lucky the £2 coin might hit one of the other muppets I've put down there for not giving me what I want!" said Bang red faced and angry!

"If you know what's good for you, you'll give my boss what he wants luv... SERIOUS!" said Thug Rock. "You'll have to kill us first" said Safa-Rhi and she spat in Thug Rock's face.

"Cheeky lil' cow, well if that's what you want... I guess it's you first luv" said Bang as he grabbed Safa-Rhi and dragged her to the edge of the bottomless pit by her hair.

"Let her go fam'" shouted Pacer as he tried to break out

of his chains and get to his sister.

Thug Rock grabbed Pacer and laughed saying "Where you going twerp?"

"Oh I aim to let her go mate hahahaha" said Bang as he dangled Safa-Rhi over the pit.

Whilst all the commotion was taking place everyone took their eye off Chunksta. Although Chunksta was frozen he was fully awake to see exactly what was going on.

Whilst frozen Chunksta was using his power to keep himself moving, this was not only to try and keep his blood flowing but he was also trying to draw all his power to break himself free, unfortunately for him up to now it wasn't working. However, now Bang had gone too far! The anger rushing through Chunksta's veins from seeing Bang's treatment of his siblings gave him a new serge of power. Unluckily for Bang, Chunksta seeing him dangling Safa-Rhi over the bottomless pit was one step too far for Chunksta to accept, he utilised that new level of strength and BOOOOOMMMMMM!!!

Chunksta smashed through the ice and smacked Thug rock right in the middle of his face launching Thug Rock across the room once again. With Thug Rock out of the picture, Chunksta released Pacer by popping off his chains and ripping the bolts out of the ground! Bang watched and laughed then called out to them "Oi Lads". They both looked up just in time to see Bang kick Safa-Rhi into the bottomless pit.

"Ahhhhhhhhhhh!" screamed Safa-Rhi as she was plunging to a sure death.

"Nooooooo!" Shouted Pacer and Chunksta.

As soon as Pacer untangled his legs from the last of the chains, he activated his suit. Bangz Army stood there astonished as they watched Pacer's Golden Beryl Gem disperse from his SG Watch and rapidly make its way to the centre of his chest to connect with his necklace whilst simultaneously wrapping Pacer's SG Suit on his body all in a matter of seconds! Chunksta followed Pacer's lead and activated his SG Suit whilst shouting "IT'S ON!!!"

Chunksta laid in to Bangz Army knocking them out one by one and two by two.

Pacer shouted to Chunksta "Handle these youts' I'm going to get Safa-Rhi".

"Don't be silly that's suicide bro, you're gonna' dead too" replied Chunksta as he threw two of Bang's soldiers through a window.

"I don't care... if that's the case we can die together!" Then Pacer used his speed and ran straight into the bottomless pit to save his sister whilst Chunksta continued to fight.

With Pacer's extraordinary speed it was only a few seconds before he caught up with his sister. Pacer used his lasers to shoot his sister free from the chains. Still falling, Safa-Rhi pressed her SG Watch and suited up.

Safa-Rhi were free, but there was still a major problem... they were still falling and as it was a bottomless pit there was no walls for Pacer to run up.

Gravity was taking its toll on them both and it was now getting harder for them to breathe. Pacer was close to passing out! A freshly suited up Safa-Rhi summoned the powers of an Eagle and grabbed her brother. Using all her power and might she gripped him tight and flew upwards.

Whilst flying in his sister's arms Pacer woke up and eventually they were both out of the pit. Safa-Rhi released Pacer from her grip in mid air and he quickly ran over to the lever then pulled it to close the pit, he then shot the lever off with his lasers in the hope that no one could ever open it again.

Safa-Rhi landed right besides Chunksta and Pacer soon joined them, however Squad Gigantic were outnumbered!

"Big and Serious, I don't know how we gonna get outta' this one" said Chunksta as more and more of Bangz Army came towards them. They were trapped with their backs against the wall as they faced off with Bangz Army, however the three teens stood firm in their fighting stances and refused to surrender.

"We fight til' the end that's what we do, this is what Jay has been preparing us for" said Safa-Rhi taking lead of her younger brothers.
"You know me, when it's on... IT'S ON!" said Chunksta as Bang, Thug Rock and Dealer parted the crowd and walked up to the front.

"That was sweet mate... pointless, but sweet... cos' now you're all gonna' die anyway!" said Bang as Thug Rock and Dealer laughed.

Safa-Rhi, Pacer and Chunksta stood side by side ready to defend and take on whatever Bang throws at them.

In an attempt to boost their confidence, Safa-Rhi looked at her brothers and said
"We got this! Remember... A drop of rain is nothing on its own, but when they form together..."

"...IT'S A STORM!!!!" Shouted Jay Gigantic as he smashed through the wall with Truth and the SG Hit Squad.

Safa-Rhi screamed with joy, "YESSSSSSSS, I knew you would make it".

"Which one of you punks wanna get it first?" said Jay as he stepped in front of the teens and transformed into Gigantic – his half Lion half human form!

Safa-Rhi, Pacer and Chunksta were shocked!

"Rah', Jay you got powers?!" said Pacer.

Jay looked back and said "When I'm in this form call me 'Gigantic', I'll explain later but right now... we got a few things to take care of".
Then Gigantic looked at Squad Gigantic and the SG Hit

Squad then commanded "GO GET EM!"

Chapter 17 - Go Get Em!

Gigantic vs Bang
Battle of the Bosses!

At this point Bang was the most confident man on Earth! Like a crazed football hooligan he shouted "LETS AVE' IT!" as Gigantic charged at him at full force. Bang was well aware that he still had Squad Gigantic out numbered even with the SG Hit Squad involved. A naive Bang made the rookie mistake of underestimating his opponent. Before he knew what hit him, he was on the floor! As Bang fell, his Soul Freezer flew out of his hand too.

Gigantic jumped on top of Bang and gave him a gruelling combo, hitting him with hard blows after blows. Punches followed by elbows and elbows followed by knees! It was a masterclass in close combat. It was too easy, eventually Gigantic jumped off Bang and taunted him "Get up and fight me like a man!"

Bang stayed down all battered and torn up, however he was still rude enough to spit blood out of his mouth and reply "That's rich coming from you, you came to the party as a bloomin' Lion!" mocking Gigantic's new appearance.

Bang slowly stood up and got in a stance to continue the fight, but as soon as he found his balance he cowardly ran behind his army and blurted out "Don't just stand there... GET HIM!" Forcing them to attack and take his revenge on Gigantic for the humiliating beating he had just received.

Gigantic braced himself for an onslaught and stepped forward to take on at least fifty of Bang's men, then suddenly he felt a hand across his chest. It was Santago who was still gleefully grinning from witnessing the beat down Gigantic just dished out to Bang.

As Santago's face got serious, he told Gigantic "This is what we're here for, go get that wimp... we'll make light work of these toy soldiers!"
They spudded' fists then Santago and the SG Hit Squad laid into Bangz Army.

Bang was scared as he couldn't see where his Soul Freezer fell to and after receiving that ferocious combination from Gigantic, he knew he couldn't match the strength he was facing.
Bang cowardly ran as fast as he could in the hope to get to a section on the far side of the building where he had previously hid the other Soul Freezer in case of an emergency just like this one!

Gigantic didn't ease up on him at all, he chased Bang all the way to the other section and unknowingly managed to grab Bang about ten metres away from where the Soul Freezer was located.

Bang's only hope was Dealer and Thug Rock as his remaining soldiers were preoccupied in a battle of their own with the SG Hit Squad. Unfortunately for Bang, his luck went from bad to worse as two other fights both involving Thug Rock and Dealer also broke out simultaneously to his clash with Gigantic.

Bangz Army vs SG Hit Squad

Bangz Army were no match for the SG Hit Squad. It was actually embarrassing, plus having Pacer and Safa-Rhi fighting alongside the SG Hit Squad made if even worse for them... Bangz Army were getting their behinds handed to them! Santago and his men were heavily outnumbered by at least three to one but still managed to go through Bangz Army like a hot knife through butter. Bang sent the signal for more back up and they came flooding in, but even with extra back up Bangz Army still had no chance against Santago's twenty men! The SG Hit Squad were a different calibre of fighters. They lived and breathed to defend and protect. Santago trained his warriors to the highest standards. Every day they went through the most gruesome cardiovascular sessions on the peaks of Paradise Mountains. They trained at high altitudes with a lack of oxygen, then they would go on to spar with the toughest men from the Tribe Of Strength before finishing the day developing flexibility, balance and power skills with Shaolin Masters.

Originally Bangz Army were a force to be reckoned with; they were ruthless mercenaries who specialised in warfare and military combat! But nowadays Bang's men were lucky to get a day in the MMA gym followed by shooting practice! Bang got slack when he came back to London and this showed on his army. The most serious of the fighters noticed the negative change and went AWOL. This left Bang heavily relying on untrained gang members who were previously from "Da Grabberz". The main soldiers remaining were previously fighting machines but had now become complacent from being way too comfortable running around terrorising everyday civilians. Facing a force as strong as the SG Hit Squad was about to be a real wake up call that they were not expecting or even half way ready for.

The SG Hit Squad destroyed Bangz Army without the use of any automatic weapons, just an array of fighting techniques and the odd Chain, Nun Chucks and Iron Staffs. The SG Hit Squad were trained in stealth and mastered the art of hitting without being hit, Safa-Rhi used a variety of animals which made her too strong for Bangz Army and Pacer was so fast that he was barely seen!

Bangz Army could hardly touch them, eventually one of them shouted to his fellow soldiers "How do you fight something you can't see?" Another replied, "You can't... this is a madness... we're droppin' like flies! Let's get out of here!" Then the majority of Bangz Army surrendered and dispersed from the battle so they could live to see another day.

As Bangz Army retreated, Santago stopped Safa-Rhi and Pacer from giving chase wisely telling them "Don't chase them, you never fight someone who doesn't want to fight you... humbly accept your victory" Safa-Rhi smiled in awe of Santago's wisdom. Santago then went on to say "This is what happens when a leader is a coward... he breeds more cowards hahahahaha". Pacer and Safa-Rhi laughed with Santago, they were star struck and amazed to be in his presence as they hadn't seen him since they were children.

In his best spoken voice ever, Pacer looked Santago straight in his eyes and said "It's an honour to stand by your side in battle".

"Pacer, you lot are the Chosen Ones, the honour is all mine" replied Santago as he bowed to Pacer and Safa-Rhi.

As the area cleared out Santago looked around and said "I think our work here is done".

"I think so too, we can take it from here big man" replied Safa-Rhi as she summoned the power of an Ox and ran out to finish off the remaining fighters who didn't flee.

"It's a pleasure to see how you've all grown, remember any time you need us we are here at your service… send my regards to the others and I'm sure we will meet again" said Santago as he followed his warriors and jumped in to their truck. As the SG Hit Squad drove off into the night a majestical portal made of multicoloured gems shot down from the sky, Pacer stood there gobsmacked as he watched their truck disappear into it. Astonished by what he just witnessed, Pacer grabbed his head with both hands and spun around shouting "MAADDDDD!" then he quickly pulled himself back together and joined Safa-Rhi in battle.

Thug Rock vs Chunksta

The Power Brawl!

Thug Rock stepped forward to engage in battle and yet again found himself confronted by Chunksta!

"God's really answering my prayers today ennit'" said Thug Rock.

"Well I guess he owes you after giving you such a

butters' face" replied Chunksta.

"Funny how people are confident after giving someone a cheap shot" said Thug Rock.
"Cheap shot? What time was that, the first or second time I folded you G?" replied a brazen Chunksta
"Well I guess its third time lucky for me lil' man" said Thug Rock as he clinched his first and swung a thunderous right hook at Chunksta.

The punch connected and sent Chunksta back a few metres. There was so much power in the punch that the floor cracked and a mini path of rubble piled up behind Chunksta's feet. Chunksta didn't go to ground but he was hurt and for the first time in his life Chunksta was startled!
Chunksta quickly shook it off then laughed saying "Yes big man finally you showed some balls... big mistake though cos' now I can't go easy on you!"

Their powers combined was too much for the building to hold, they were trading blows that sent each other through brick walls and even steel beams. This was a true heavy weight clash, only God knows how the building didn't collapse there and then!
As Chunksta charged into Thug Rock, Thug Rock shot an array of rocks and mini boulders from his fist into Chunksta's path.
"Hold some rock shots rude boy" shouted Thug Rock as he continued to blast.

Chunksta punched through each and every one of them, effortlessly smashing them into smithereens as he replied "Is that what you call them? More like pebbles G hahahaha".

As soon as Chunksta got close enough, he rugby tackled Thug Rock causing them both to fly through a brick wall and end up outside. The pair continued fighting in the car park launching cars and forklifts at each other. They were creating a massive scene which now made people appear. More and more spectators arrived and began filming the fight on their phones then posting it on social media sites.

One brave but stupid spectator couldn't resist missing the opportunity for likes and views, so he got dangerously close to the battle just to get a good position to record Snaps of the fight.
"Yoooo, mans' out 'ere... war settings, watching man like Squad Gigantic deal with the Ops'... OOHHHHHH SHHHHH.....!!!"

Out of no where Chunksta came flying at the Snapper in mid air! Luckily the Snapchatting spectator dropped his phone and ducked just in time, narrowly saving himself from a catastrophic collision with Chunksta who Thug Rock ruthlessly grabbed and threw across the car park at full speed!
Chunksta smashed into a Lorry head first, before he even landed and had a chance to take a breath Thug Rock send at least eight rocks that blammed into his chest.
Eventually Chunksta got back on his feet and threw a white van at Thug Rock in retaliation to the Rock Shots! It was a real mess, both guys were giving as good as they got and even though they were both battered and bruised none of them were giving up.

Meanwhile inside the building, Truth locked eyes with Dealer.

Truth vs Dealer

Battle of the Minds!

Truth grabbed Dealer and gave him a knee to the stomach, cleverly knocking the wind out of him. He then followed it up with a swift three punch combo... Left Jab... Right Hook... Left Uppercut! Striking Dealer to the ground. As Truth stood over Dealer, Dealer swiftly swept him off his feet. As Truth went down he banged his head on a random plank of wood.

Dealer got himself together whilst Truth was hurt, he brushed of his soft unbuckled leather jacket whilst saying "Show some respect, this is designer I'll have you know". The forever flashy Dealer then went on to say "You obviously don't know who you're messing with do you? Do you really know what I'm on?".

With the intent to show Truth exactly what he was on, Dealer gripped on his King of Hearts card. Immediately the card started to cluster up and release a white glow as he walked towards Truth.

The fact of the matter was Dealer didn't actually know who he was dealing with and what level Truth was on! Truth's mind was way too strong for Dealer to control. The Chosen Ones were naturally born with their SG Gemstones, whereas Thug Rock and Dealer's gemstones were intertwined into their DNA through special circumstances. The SG Gems are also the most powerful gems known to mankind as they draw a high power potency that is literally from out of this World!

This meant that the Chosen Ones' powers were stronger than Thug Rock and Dealer's. The SG Gems spirit and force derives from an ancient power source greater than this World, the average human can not survive this force running through their blood... they can barely survive the force of weaker Dark Gems! The force chooses it's inhabitants through the ancestral bloodline of ancient warriors and protectors of the universe who's DNA is strong enough to house the spirit and force; this is why they are referred to as the 'Chosen Ones'.

The spirit and force that runs through the SG Gems has the ability to suppress weaker gems if a cosmic battle of gems is to ever to occur.

As soon as Dealer tried to control Truth's mind, Truth was able to read the play and take control of the situation. Truth laughed to himself then went on to pretend that Dealer's attempt was working.
"You're not the only one with special powers hahahaha. Rule one... never underestimate you're opponent!" said a confident Dealer.
Then he told Truth "Look into my eyes". Truth played along and looked in to his eyes.

Dealer went on to say "Good boy, from now on I rule you! Bow to your King and serve him".
Dealer felt untouchable, he was so arrogant that he didn't realised that Truth's eyes did not change like the Yeti's did!

Truth cunningly went on to one knee and said "My King, how can I serve you?"

Dealer stood directly over Truth and said "You will know when the time is right, now bow!"

Truth dropped his head to bow, then he made a sudden stop and began to slowly raise his head with a smile. Dealer was confused, "What are you doing? I said Bow to me!" he shouted.

Truth carried on smiling and shook his head to say 'no'. Dealer didn't know what was going on, he thought to himself 'why isn't he obeying me?'

Truth stayed on his knee and looked up starring directly into Dealer's eyes, then said "You said it yourself, rule number one... never underestimate your opponent!"

Then POOOOOWWWWWWW!!!!!
Truth gave Dealer a rising uppercut that lifted him off the ground and launched him into the air! Before Dealer even had the chance to land, Truth followed up with a devastating over hand punch to his chest sending Dealer right back down to the ground.

Dealer was KO'd! Truth gripped him by his leather jacket that he loved so much and dragged him over to the same corner where the teens were chained up earlier.

The Power Brawl continued....

Whilst Truth was handling Dealer, Chunksta and Thug Rock were still going at it in the car park! Chunksta managed to back Thug Rock into a corner.

BLUKU... BAM... BLLAAAAAWWWWW! Chunksta was

giving Thug Rock a sweet blend of explosive blows, forcing Thug Rock to the ground.

Thug Rock had no reply to Chunksta's brutal attack, he had nothing left in him as he sprawled out on the floor looking battered and defeated.

Chunksta was also tired and fatigued. Realising his opponent was down and out he drew a deep breath of relief and then gloated saying "I guess that's three nil now ugly face".

Chunksta laughed as he turned his back on Thug Rock and slowly walked away. As he hobbled along he looked ahead and saw Safa-Rhi coming towards him.

Still a little distance away from her brother, Safa-Rhi sarcastically shouted "Could you make any more of a mess?"

"Shut up!" shouted Chunksta using his last piece of energy. He wasn't in the mood for jokes, he was knackered.

Chunksta thought the battle was over and with Safa-Rhi's jokes distracting him, he made the silly mistake of not concentrating on his enemy! This gave Thug Rock the perfect opportunity to get himself together and use his last piece of strength to muster up the biggest Rock Shot he had ever created!

Safa-Rhi was bussin' up at how tired her brother was. She laughed so hard that her eyes closed whilst she bent over holding her belly. She finally finished cackling and lifted her head just in time to see Thug Rock propel the mega Rock Shot at Chunksta!

"DUUCCKKK!" Shouted Safa-Rhi to her brother, but her

warning came too late. The mega Rock Shot smashed into Chunksta's back at a vicious speed and dropped him.

Safa-Rhi was furious! Instantly she summoned the power of a Rhino and charged at Thug Rock taking him down! As soon as Thug Rock hit the deck Safa-Rhi summoned the power of a Silverback Gorilla and started to pound him.

Chunksta eventually lifted himself up and saw his sister destroying Thug Rock. He ran over and joined in the onslaught. Now Thug Rock was truly defeated and to make things worse for Thug Rock, he was defeated by a girl!

Learning from his previous mistake, Chunksta got some rest and stood guard over Thug Rock as he laid unconscious. As Safa-Rhi headed back into the building to help the rest of Squad, Pacer came over to Chunksta and gave his brother a run down of the battle with Bangz Army.

Gigantic vs Bang
Battle of the Bosses... Continued!

Gigantic flung Bang to the other side of the room. As soon as Bang landed, Gigantic let out a massive ROOOOOAAAAAR! Then followed through with a solid push kick to the chest knocking the wind out of Bang. Without giving Bang a second to catch his breath, Gigantic lifted him with his left hand and tossed him into the air, then smashed him across his jaw with an unforgiving right hook as he came back down!

Bang was getting torn to shreds. His suit was great

against guns and explosions but it was no help against Gigantic's raw strength. Bang's chance of survival ultimately depended on him getting to his Soul Freezer as his nemesis wasn't letting up!

Gigantic grabbed Bang and held him up by his cheeks. He pushed Bang's face up against his Fire Red Diamond and said "Open your eyes rude boy, LOOK AT IT!!! This is the closest you'll ever get to the gems!"

"That's what you think mate" laughed Bang as he struggled to get out of Gigantic's grip.
"Stop talking crap and do your worst mate. We all know you ain't got what it takes to finish me off! That's always been your problem- your hearts too clean, Mr Nice guy ain't ya" taunted Bang.

This really wound Gigantic up and that's exactly what Bang wanted. He knew his hidden Soul Freezer was situated on the other side of the room and the only way he was going to get there was if Gigantic put him there.

Gigantic let out another massive "ROOOAAAAARRRRRR!!!" then once again tossed Bang into the air like a doll. Whilst Bang was mid-air, Gigantic drew his arm back as far as he could... then "BLLLLAAAAOOOOWWWW"
He delivered a disgustingly hard full bodied punch straight to Bang's gut which sent Bang soaring into a metal beam on the other side of the room. Bang slowly slid down the beam looking dead to the World. Gigantic took a moment to compose himself in order to avoid doing something he would later regret. Bang was right, Gigantic didn't have the heart to kill him but at this

particular moment of time his mixed emotions of anger, betrayal and even a touch of fear was getting the better of him.

Bang was down and out. Gigantic thought there was no way he was going to get back up from that. However Bang's alien technology suit shot a force of adrenalin like energy into Bang which enabled him to slowly pick himself up. As Bang stood up he realised Gigantic put him exactly where he needed to be... Bang was literally on top of his hidden Soul Freezer.

Even though his body was riddled with pain, Bang still saw the positive and slowly grinned to himself thinking 'Finally somethings gone my way'.

Bang grabbed the Soul Freezer whilst Gigantic's back was turned and fired a Grenade at Gigantic shouting "Oi pussy cat... ave' some of this!"

Gigantic spun round just at the right time and slapped away the Grenade that came towards him. BOOOOOOMMMMMMMMMM! The Grenade's path was changed and it exploded in the opposite corner of the room which was directly above Truth and Dealer!

Truth was half way through chaining Dealer to a pillar whilst the explosion happened. Truth looked up to see a small section of the ceiling coming down on him, he tried to move out of the way but wasn't quick enough. A sharp edged steel pole plunged into the right side of Truth's chest smashing through his rib cage and piercing his lungs. Truth collapsed whilst gasping for breath, Dealer took this opportunity to begin untangling himself with the hope of making a run for it before the building fully caved in!

Bang continued his attack sending a flurry of Freeze and Burn shots followed by a Grenade! This wasn't smart. The building's foundations were already weakened from Thug Rock and Chunksta's battle and Bang's Grenade explosions wasn't helping at all. It was only a matter of time before the whole building came tumbling down.

Gigantic managed to dodge Bang's attempts but he couldn't get close to him. Gigantic guarded himself well but he knew it was only a matter of time before Bang's shots would connect.

Eventually Bang's efforts paid off. A burn shot hit Gigantic and pushed him back, then a Grenade explosion immediately followed and blasted Gigantic out of a window! He landed in the car park where Pacer, Safa-Rhi and Thug Rock were situated.

Bang finally hit Gigantic, but it came at a cost! The building was now on its last legs and Bang needed to escape or he was going to be a victim of his own detonations.

When Gigantic fell out of the sky, he landed right in front of Safa-Rhi as she was running back to the building.

"Are you ok?" asked a concerned Safa-Rhi. "I'm good luv' this is a minor" said a groggy Gigantic trying to play down his pain so Safa-Rhi didn't worry. Gigantic and Safa-Rhi both looked at the building as it was slowly falling apart.

"We need to get out of here. Where's your brothers and The Hit Squad?" said Gigantic.

"The Hit Squad's gone, they defeated Bangz Army and left. Chunkz and Pacer are over there and I thought Truth might have been with you!?!" replied Safa-Rhi as she began to worry for her brother.

"He must still be inside... connect and tell him to come now!" said Gigantic.

Safa-Rhi tried to connect with her brother, the connection was weak but she could feel something was there.
"Bro where are you?" Said Safa-Rhi telepathically.

Truth was on the floor in a really bad way. There was no reply, so Safa-Rhi asked again "TRUTH, where are you?!"

The second attempt was more successful. She managed to get through to her brother but Truth's response was feeble, he only managed to force out a few words "Help sis... I'm... inside... and... I can't... breathe....... ground floor".

"He's inside and he's hurt" said Safa-Rhi as she began to panic.
"Take Pacer and get him now" said Gigantic.

Safa-Rhi shouted to Pacer "Pacer, Truth's inside and he's hurt! We need to get him now".
Pacer zoomed into the building and started searching for his brother but he didn't know where he should be looking.
Safa-Rhi followed behind by borrowing the speed of a Cheetah and she headed directly for the ground floor.

Chunksta rushed over to be with Gigantic forgetting about Thug Rock.

Thug Rock eventually woke up and found himself alone, he looked ahead and saw Chunksta with Gigantic. Thug Rock thought 'forget that' he didn't have any more fight left in him so he discreetly snuck round the back of the building to get away and live to fight another day.

Whilst this all took place Bang was also making his escape. As far as Bang was concerned both Dealer and Thug Rock were still in the crumbling building, but he didn't care! Bang selfishly aimed to save himself. He made a run for it dodging and diving over falling debris, his easiest way out was completely blocked by steel and rubble, he had to find another route. After identifying a new path Bang ran towards the hole in the ground that he carelessly created earlier, then he jumped down to the floor beneath where him and Gigantic's battle began.

Bang looked to his left and saw his other Soul Freezer, then he looked to his right and saw Truth on the floor with his SG Gem gleaming! Dealer was just behind Truth still trying to get out of the chains.

"Bang I'm glad to see you, help me... I'm all tangled up mate" said Dealer.

The building was getting worse and the ceiling was beginning to fall even more, they all literally had seconds to get away or risk being crushed by the plummeting building. Bang had what should be a simple decision to make: Help his friend Dealer and escape together or grab his other Soul Freezer Gun and Truth's SG Gem then escape with both prized possessions.

As Bang was battling with himself trying to make a decision, Safa-Rhi and Pacer both came running in from different entrances, they both saw their brother on the floor and ran over to him. This made Bang's decision much easier, the deal had now changed: Save Dealer or retrieve his Soul Freezer and kill three members of Squad Gigantic whilst taking their gems.

Without any second thought or hesitation Bang picked up his other Soul Freezer then looked over at Dealer and the teens, with both weapons in hand he aimed the Soul Freezers at them with the intention of turning them to ashes with Burn shots.

Bang said "Sorry Dealer it's everyman for themselves".

Just as Bang went to press the trigger, Pacer sped over to him and side-kicked his shins causing him to fall forwards on to the ground. Bang's shot missed everyone and hit the already unstable ceiling beam above. Now the building was definitely coming down!

Bang got to his feet and ran out the back of the building to save himself, leaving his 'so called' friend Dealer for dead as what was left of the ceiling above and everything that rested on it came thundering down! All the spectators dispersed and ran for safety. Pacer ran back with the intention of removing his brother and sister from harms way! Pacer was fast enough to get back to them but he wasn't fast enough to remove himself and his siblings from disaster- the three storey building collapsed right on top of them!

Somehow through all the madness Dealer managed to save his own life. He broke free from his chains and escaped from the building just before it collapsed.

Dealer was enraged! Everything Elisha told him about Bang's character was true, he couldn't trust Bang as far as he could throw him! Not only did he leave him for dead, he even pulled the trigger to cause his death! From that moment on Dealer made his main purpose in life to destroy Bang!

Bang saved himself not caring about what may come of Thug Rock and Dealer. To the best of Bang's knowledge both Thug Rock and Dealer were still in the building fighting for their lives and that's if they were lucky! He looked back and saw the whole building fall. "There's no way they're surviving that. I guess that's the end of Thug Rock and Dealer... ah well was nice knowing them" Bang heartlessly said to himself as he hot stepped through the back area of the buildings car park. Then to Bang's surprise, he heard a shout "Bang, quick... this way!" It was Thug Rock.

Thug Rock was oblivious to what just took place inside between Bang and Dealer. He asked Bang "Where's Dealer, is he good?"

Bang looked at Thug Rock and lied to him.

"Yeah he's pukka', I saw him on my way out. He said to get you and meet him back at the spot".

"Cool lets go, I got a whip just a couple roads up" said Thug Rock. Then Bang and Thug Rock ran for it.

Back in the building things were looking bad for Safa-Rhi, Truth and Pacer. The whole building had now collapsed on top of them! Gigantic and Chunksta stood outside powerless forced to watch it all happen.

"NOOOOOOOOOOO!!!" shouted Gigantic

Gigantic and Chunksta ran to the building that was now just a piece of its foundation surrounded by wreckage, rubble and dust. They both ran over and went through all the wreckage inch by inch trying to find the other teens. They turned every stone in their path and tossed every piece of heavy steel they came across but still couldn't find their family members. This was a massive three storey warehouse, two pair of arms weren't enough to get through all of this building's remains.

Thinking the worst Chunksta was close to breaking down and giving up.
"They're dead, they're dead! My brothers and sister are gone!" Chunksta frantically shouted with his eyes welling up.

Gigantic grabbed him by his arms and told him "Stop talking Rubbish! Get yourself together, they're alive I can feel it… we just gotta' dig deeper! I need you to be strong! Right now we're all we got… OK".
"Cool big man, I got you" replied Chunksta as they gripped hands and pulled each other in for a hug. "You search this side and I'll do over there OK!" said Gigantic
As they went off to continue the search, Chunksta saw slight movement in the rubble.
"Gigantic come here quick!" shouted Chunksta.

Gigantic came running over and they both dug into the ruins, effortlessly throwing steel beams and concrete slabs as if they were feather pillows.
They removed what had to be at least thirty to forty

tons of debris. As they got down to the final pieces, Safa-Rhi burst out the rubble with her brothers in her hands.

Luckily when the building came tumbling down Safa-Rhi used her intelligence and drew the power of a Dung Beetle; an animal able to carry 1141 times of their own body weight. As a human equivalent this gave Safa-Rhi the ability to carry at least sixty tons on her back. She used her powers and quickly dragged her brothers under her body and protected them from the devastation until Gigantic and Chunksta found them… Safa-Rhi's quick thinking saved their lives.

"Truth isn't breathing… HELP!!" she shouted as Pacer stood up and dusted himself off.

Gigantic and Chunksta was amazed! How were they still alive? How were they even walking?
Gigantic hugged them and said "How?"

"I'll explain everything later, but right now we need to help Truth. He's gone pale and he isn't breathing!" said Safa-Rhi.
Gigantic made contact with Tanya as he grabbed Truth and took him away from the demolished building.

"T, can you hear me babes?" said Gigantic.
"Yep I've heard everything" said Tanya as she cried through the comms.
"I need a report on Truth's health ASAP" replied Gigantic.
"It's not good babes" said Tanya as her cry got louder.

"He's suffered a lot of trauma. It appears that his lungs have been punctured for at least 15 minutes. This has restricted his ability to breathe and I'm afraid he's..." Then Tanya took a deep long pause.

"You're afraid he's what? Don't say it!" replied Gigantic. "He's DEAD!!!" Screamed Tanya as she burst into tears.

Everyone was listening through their comms. Chunksta reacted first and started smashing everything around him out of anger.

"I'M GONNA' KILL BANG! WHERE IS HE?!" shouted Chunksta, but Bang was long gone.

Pacer sat in one place and cried. He didn't even have it in him to be angry, he was just shocked and lost. Gigantic came out of Lion form and held Truth in his arms cursing the universe for making this happen to him.

"He's a Chosen One, this isn't in the prophecy. How, how... Hooowww?!" bellowed Jay confused as to how this could've happened.

Then Safa-Rhi slowly placed her arm on Jay's shoulder and calmingly said "Lay him flat on the floor". The calm humbleness in Safa-Rhi's voice had an aura which made Jay feel compelled to oblige without asking a single question.

Safa-Rhi stepped forward and leaned over her brother. Then she opened her hand and placed it about two inches above his heart. As she did this her Pink Star Diamond started to glow, so did Truth's Purple Star Diamond. Safa-Rhi's eyes turned pink and the glow from her Pink Star Diamond travelled from her SG Gem into her chest then through her shoulders, down her arms, out of her palm and into her brother's heart. Miraculously Truth's cut healed up and he was no longer bleeding, but he still laid there unresponsive and unfortunately dead.

Safa-Rhi stood up and looked down at her brother begging the universe saying "Please make this work, Pleeaassse!"

Everybody stood back awestruck by what had just happened, they weren't sure what Safa-Rhi had just done. Did she help her brother or did she perform a farewell ritual? Then suddenly Safa-Rhi fell into Jay's arms and broke down into tears.

"It didn't work" she cried.

"What didn't work sweet heart?" said Jay.

Then Safa-Rhi went on to tell a story from when they were children in Paradise Mountains:

"Once when we were young kids in Ipharadisi Inzintaba... not too long before you took us. Me and my brother snuck to what they called the forbidden area and played games. We were warned by our parents not to go there as this section of the Mountains were deemed too dangerous for children to climb. However me and Raheem were mischievous and inquisitive so we disobeyed and went there anyway.

We were playing a game of 'Tag' and after running away from Raheem I found myself on the edge of a boulder. It wasn't the edge of a major cliff or anything but there was still a drop of about fifteen to twenty metres. Raheem got closer to me and was just about to make me 'it' and instead of telling him to stop because where I was standing was dangerous, I got caught up in the game and summoned the reflex of a Cat to dodge his attempt to tag me. I used the Cat's reflex and side stepped Raheem. Raheem lost his footing and feel off the Boulder. I managed to use the same Cat powers to jump down to help him, but he was already dead. As I hugged and cried over him I noticed a glow leave my body and go into Raheem, then magically Raheem woke up. When he woke up he was dazed but he was still normal as if nothing even happened... no injuries, no nothing!

I was hoping that the same thing would've happened just then, but it hasn't and now Raheem's gone forever!" said Safa-Rhi as she continued to bawl her eyes out.

Whilst Jay tried to comfort Safa-Rhi and her remaining brothers, Safa-Rhi miraculously felt a strange feeling of relief in her heart. Then she heard a voice in her mind say,

"Stop being a drama queen, you can't get rid of me that easily!" It was Truth!

He telepathically spoke to his sister letting her know it worked and he was still alive.

"Raheeeeeemmmm!" shouted Safa-Rhi in joy.

Everyone looked over at Truth, he coughed and let out a deep breath. Truth was alive! Safa-Rhi healed him and brought him back from death's door.

Safa-Rhi, Pacer and Chunksta ran and jumped on to their brother.

"I thought we lost you bro" said Chunksta.

"If you lot don't get off me now, you're really gonna'

lose me... especially you Chunkz" said Truth trying to breathe as his brothers and sister smothered him.

"T, he's back!" shouted Jay to Tanya through the comms.
"I know hun and I've done a full check on his vitals and they're all fine... It's a madness, it's a miracle!" said Tanya.
"For real, you don't know the half... I'll explain later luv'" said Jay.
"That was MAADD!" said Truth, then he shook his head and started laughing like no one had ever seen him laugh before.

Seeing Truth laugh surprised Jay and the teens, they were flabbergasted. Truth hardly ever smiled, let alone release a big of round laughter.

As a joke Pacer asked his brother "You sure you're alright fam'?"
Truth replied, "Shut up man" whilst ruffling his little brother's hair.
"Less of the jokes, where's Bang?" said Truth.
"He's long gone and so should we be!" replied Jay.

"Bang and his eediot' army got a good taste of Squad Gigantic's capabilities. I know there's going to be bigger and badder battles to come, but after that beating, I don't think we're gonna' be hearing from them for a while!" said Jay proud of his squad.
"Plus after what Bang did to Dealer, I think he's got his own problems he's gonna' have to deal with!" said Pacer.

"You're gonna' have to fill me in on that one later youngen, but right now we gotta get outta ere" said Jay. Jay transformed back into Gigantic to protect his identity on the way back to HQ.

Gigantic and Chunksta jumped on his SG Quad Bike whilst Truth and Safa-Rhi jumped on Truth's SG1000 with Pacer running alongside them.

People began to filter back into the area and filmed with their smartphones as Squad Gigantic dispersed from the scene after winning their first major battle.

Chapter 18 - There's Always Sunshine After Rain

"Hi I'm Sandra Patty and this is the London News".
The theme song to the news played and woke up Jay.
It was the morning after the mayhem and Tanya had
already woke the teens for school and sixth form but as
Jay's diary was clear, she decided to leave him to sleep.

As Jay woke up and wiped the matter from the
corner of his eyes, Sandra Patty the London news
reporter went on to say:

*"Today's head line news: Rumble on the Docks! Last
night a total of 16 local business owners and workers
from the docks reported a major disturbance coming
from a derelict building in the area. This disturbance saw
explosions that caused the building to collapse into
nothing but rubble, with the majority of the building
bizarrely disappearing into what can only be described
as a near bottomless pit! It was truly like something
from the movies... We dread to think what or even who
else may have been sucked in to the devastating
anomalous hole.*
*London City Police attended the scene and apprehended
a large number of the infamous organised crime group
'Bangz Army'.*
*No one knows the full extent of what took place to lead
to this local catastrophe, however recovered CCTV
footage before the major blast took place showed a
number of violent clashes between Squad Gigantic and
Bangz Army.*

In a statement made by the Mayor earlier he promised a full investigation will take place led by the City Police with full backing from his office. The Mayor went on to thank Squad Gigantic for bringing whatever took place to a halt and delivering a number of wanted criminals to the arms of justice.

Earlier I took a look at the actual site where it all went down and I have to be honest, as much respect as I have for the Mayor, I think it's time he opens his eyes. Yes the Squad Gigantic have foiled a number of crimes and some would argue that they have made London safer... I get that, but at what cost to London's citizens and tax payers. Squad Gigantic can't continue to have this 'get out of jail free card' that allows them to do whatever they want without consequences. We thank you for protecting the City, but maybe... just maybe it's time they answer for a few things too! This is Sandra Patty reporting live from the Docks for the London News. Have a great day and whatever you do, be safe".

Jay went downstairs and saw the rest of the household were also watching the news whilst they ate breakfast.

"What's wrong with this 'Ms Chatty Patty' chick? I swear down when I see her I'm gonna' box her, she's always got some foolishness to say" said Safa-Rhi.

Tanya and Jay laughed at Safa-Rhi's feistiness.

"It's true we risk everything daily to protect the endz' and she wanna' talk like that" added Chunksta.
"She's just a bitter hater with nothing else to do" said Truth.

"You lot got time if you're paying her any mind, you know how the ting' goes; happy chicks ain't hating and hating chicks ain't happy. She's just trying to keep her job and make a story at any cost" said Truth making every one in the room erupt with laughter.

"This is why it's essential to stay disciplined and keep our identity hidden, it's a cold World so for whatever reason not everybody will see the benefits we bring. People will always have things to say- sometimes good, sometimes bad. Ignore all of them- the good and the bad because nobody can't break you or make you. One thing to always remember tho', Bang and any other little ediot' enemies are out there and they'll be listening to everything that gets said whilst shaking in their boots, so it doesn't matter what people are saying just as long as they're saying something, hahahaha" laughed Jay sending a powerful message to the teens to enable them to see past rumours and gossip.

"Any way times ticking man, you lot hurry up and eat your breakfast then get to school. Oh yeah and don't think you lot got away with sneaking out yesterday! Yeah you thought I forgot hahahaha no way! Everyone except Truth is grounded for 2 weeks! You ain't leaving this house unless it's to save the World!" Enforced Jay.

"Arr man 'louw us, we defeated Bang yesterday that must count for something," said Pacer.
"'Louw you?! If you didn't sneak out yesterday none of that would've happened, remember that? Furthermore, if you carry on I can make it 4 weeks... is that want you want?" asked Jay.
"Shut up Danny" said Safa-Rhi and Chunksta fearing he

was going to make the punishment worse.

"We understand Jay and sorry for being so dum'" said Safa-Rhi.

"I'm glad some of you have got sense, anyway I'm not completely badmind. You lot have had a hard few months... years even, and finally things should calm down for a while. Remember what I always tell you; there's always sunshine after rain and even though you're grounded for 2 weeks of it, I aim to let you enjoy some of that sunshine. So me and Tanya decided we're gonna go out as a family to have some fun tonight" said Jay.

Tanya smiled whilst the teens hugged and thanked her and Jay.

Jay naively rested his guards thinking that things were finally about to calm down, but little did he know things were about to get much worse!

Chapter 19 - The Raw Deal!

Bang was at home chilling with Elisha and Thug Rock. Thug Rock was confused as to why Dealer hadn't made it back to HQ yet. However as Thug Rock was never the sharpest tool in the box he didn't over think things, to be honest the only time he ever showed an ounce of intelligence was when it involved crime and even that would still be at a minimal level! Thug Rock simply thought Dealer may have had to lay low to shake off the police.

It was about 11:30am, Bang was sat alone in his office when he heard an aggressive knock on the door.

He shouted "Who's knocking on my door like the bloody police!" He stood up checking his CCTV and saw it was Dealer. Bang jumped out of his skin, it was as if he saw a ghost!

Dealer was at the door with at least thirty of Bang's best men, Bang couldn't believe his eyes! He thought Dealer was a dead man for sure!

Knowing he was about to be exposed, Bang sat back at his desk stressing as he tried to quickly concoct a story to clear his name. He continued to ignore Dealer's knock on the door, hoping that no one else in the house would hear it either.

Luckily for Bang, Elisha was in the bedroom singing along to the 'Shape of You' remix by Ed Sheeran and Stormzy, she couldn't hear a thing as it blasted out of her Bluetooth speakers.

Unfortunately for Bang, as the door knocked Thug Rock was walking through the hallway.

"Can't no one hear the door?!" shouted Thug Rock as he went to open it.

"I thought I heard something" said Elisha as she muted the volume on her speakers and walked towards the hallway.

Thug Rock opened the door to see Dealer.

"YOOOOO bro it's about time, what happened to you? I thought you were a goner' when you didn't meet us back here last night" said Thug Rock to Dealer.

"I should be asking what happened to you bro, you look messed up!" replied Dealer looking at Thug Rock who was filled with cuts and bruises all over.

"It's nothing bro, rough day at the office... you know how it goes, you look like you took a couple slaps too" said Thug Rock.

"What you talking bout' anyway? Who told you I was coming back here last night? Lucky I even came back here at all!" said Dealer becoming angry.

"Bang said you were gonna' meet us here last night when we escaped that madness" said Thug Rock looking slightly confused.

"Hahaha he would say that. Where is he? Elisha beautiful, be a sweet heart and tell him to come out here please" said Dealer.

"Why don't you come in?" replied Elisha.

"Nar, never again! As you said he ain't who he claims to be" said Dealer.

Elisha smiled and gladly walked off to get Bang, finally her plan was falling into place.

"What's going on?" said Thug Rock.
"You'll find out in a second bro" said Dealer.

Bang came out frantically waving his Soul Freezer around.
"What d'you want you little toe rag?! You got some bloody nerve coming to my spot tooled up with a bunch of goons- my goons at that! Silly move boy... silly move" said Bang to Dealer.
Dealer laughed then said "I've got some nerve?! This is coming from the geezer who not only left his so called right hand man for dead, he also fired the shot that could've killed him! No you got the cheek to tell me I've got a nerve!"

"WHAT?!" said Thug Rock hearing the truth of what happened last night.
"Not even those scummy Squad Gigantic guys left me for dead! I knew something weren't right when we left, you're a wrongen' Bang!" said Thug Rock.

"Arr shut up you idiot, it wasn't exactly hard to fool you was it? You ain't got one piece of sense in that head of yours! Without me you're nothing, that goes for both of you! If it weren't for me you'd be little orphans living in the mountains, remember that!" responded Bang.

"Whatever mate, you keep telling yourself that Bang, we put in all the work not you. You had your first proper fight last night and now look at you- black and blue from head to toe. He humiliated you" said Dealer.

As they were talking no one noticed that Elisha left

the hallway, she went upstairs and picked up some bags that she had previously packed. After her conversation with Dealer at the Ace Of Clubs, she knew this day would eventually come and she wanted to make sure she was ready.

Elisha came back downstairs with her designer luggage and said "Dealer I'm coming with you hun" then she kissed Dealer on the lips and looked back at Bang saying "You're washed mate. Someone needs to put you in a dryer! You've had your time now you're a defeated man. Without that gun and those Dark Gems you're nothing but a selfish bitter powerless man".

"Yeah, but you're forgetting a few things treacle. I do have this gun and all those men standing behind you are on my payroll. I don't need none of you! I built this, all of this. Lads attack em!" commanded Bang.

"Oh yeah about that too, these guys standing here are my guys now. D'you really think they're going to take orders from a loser like you now they've seen your true colours. Sure you've got half of your army left, a bunch of fools whose loyalty to you can't be broken. It's quite honourable actually but these guys and a lot more are now with me. They're no longer Bangz army, they're Spade Gang!" Said Dealer.

"That's a load of rubbish!" said Bang.
"Is it? Maybe I should show you" laughed Dealer, then he stepped back and sent his command "Spade Gang, disarm him".

The Spade Gang ambushed Bang and took the Soul Freezer from him. One of Dealer's men carried the Soul

Freezer to him and said "I guess this is yours now boss".
Dealer took the Soul Freezer and said "Yeah, I guess it
is".

Bang shouted and screamed telling Dealer, Thug
Rock and Elisha "You'll pay for this, I guarantee it...
you're all nothing without me!"
Dealer laughed and said "Blah blah blah, alright mate".
Then he sent his Spade Gang into the HQ to take any
items they felt was needed for the new Spade Gang HQ
at the Ace Of Clubs.

Elisha went to Bang's secret safe to take his Dark
Gem's. Luckily for Bang he changed the location of the
majority of his gems to another secret safe in the HQ,
but Elisha still managed to take a few of them and give
to Dealer. Dealer smiled as Elisha gave him what looked
like at least £1million in cash and a bag of gems from
Bang's Safe.
"These are some of those precious stones that mean the
World to you aren't they? To me they have no value,
I've already got powers. However just knowing that they
mean so much to you I think I'll take them!" said a
vindictive Dealer.

Bang was becoming even angrier now, he continued
to send threats whilst a few of Dealer's Spade Gang
members held him.
Dealer was just about to leave Bang's HQ with Thug
Rock and Elisha, then Bang shouted "You'll pay for this!
I'm gonna kill you both. I'm gonna' send you both to
meet your weak, stupid, good for nothing dead parents
who deserted you!"
This struck a nerve with Dealer who stopped in his

tracks and told his gang members to let Bang go. "That's what I thought" said Bang as he straightened his shirt. "You thought what?" said Dealer, then he blasted Bang with a Freeze shot from the Soul Freezer.
"I think you need to chill out mate" said Dealer.
Everyone laughed and they left the Bang HQ.

Bang stood there frozen and helpless. It was probably a good thing that he had been frozen as he had a lot to think about.
Once he thawed out he decided he was going to rebuild his whole army and go to war with Thug Rock and Dealer as well as Squad Gigantic!

The Streets were about to get crazier than they'd ever been!

Thug rock and Dealer sat in the back of a blacked out 4x4 whilst Elisha drove.
"What you gonna' do now bro?" said Dealer to Thug Rock.
Then he went on to say, "There's a space for you here with me, right at the top side by side. None of that follow the leader rubbish like Bang had it".

"I respect that bro, but honestly this is your ting'. You don't need me in it, you got a gang now. You can use your powers to make them rob and steal everything in the World for you bro. You're good, you don't need me in it and honestly I think it's time for me to start my own thing too. I'ma' build Rock Hard to be the biggest security firm in the UK extorting and forcing everyone to use our services".

Dealer laughed and Elisha also had a grin. She was happy to hear Thug Rock wanted to go his own way so she could have Dealer all to herself.

"Well know you've always got a brother in me bro" said Dealer to Thug Rock.
"That's vice versa G', I got you!" Replied Thug Rock. "I'm sure we'll link on a few jobs real soon anyway" said Dealer.
They both laughed and drove off to their business premises.

London and the rest of the UK were about to face a danger that they had never seen before, a danger that would spread worldwide... and even further! Crime sprees in abundance and turf wars that would claim many lives and universes! Bang and his army will definitely collide with the Spade Gang in the future and surely Squad Gigantic will have to go against them both... As well anything else that may come at them!

THE END.... For now!!!

SG Merchandise and much more available at:
www.SQUADGIGANTIC.com

"A Dream's Worth Nothing If You Leave It On Your Pillow...
Go Get Em!"
- Big J